A LYON OF HER OWN

The Lyon's Den Connected World

Anna St. Claire

© Copyright 2023 by Anna St. Claire
Text by Anna St. Claire
Cover by Dar Albert

Dragonblade Publishing, Inc. is an imprint of Kathryn Le Veque Novels, Inc.
P.O. Box 23
Moreno Valley, CA 92556
ceo@dragonbladepublishing.com

Produced in the United States of America

First Edition July 2023
Print Edition

Reproduction of any kind except where it pertains to short quotes in relation to advertising or promotion is strictly prohibited.

All Rights Reserved.

The characters and events portrayed in this book are fictitious. Any similarity to real persons, living or dead, is purely coincidental and not intended by the author.

ARE YOU SIGNED UP FOR DRAGONBLADE'S BLOG?

You'll get the latest news and information on exclusive giveaways, exclusive excerpts, coming releases, sales, free books, cover reveals and more.

Check out our complete list of authors, too!

No spam, no junk. That's a promise!

Sign Up Here

www.dragonbladepublishing.com

Dearest Reader;

Thank you for your support of a small press. At Dragonblade Publishing, we strive to bring you the highest quality Historical Romance from some of the best authors in the business. Without your support, there is no 'us', so we sincerely hope you adore these stories and find some new favorite authors along the way.

Happy Reading!

CEO, Dragonblade Publishing

Additional Dragonblade books by Author Anna St. Claire

The Rakes of Mayhem Series
The Earl of Excess (Book 1)
The Marquess of Mischief (Book 2)
The Duke of Disorder (Book 3)
A Gift for Agatha (Novella)

The Lyon's Den Series
Lyon's Prey
The Heart of a Lyon
A Lyon of Her Own

Also from Anna St. Claire
Once upon a Haunted Heart

Other Lyon's Den Books

Into the Lyon's Den by Jade Lee
The Scandalous Lyon by Maggi Andersen
Fed to the Lyon by Mary Lancaster
The Lyon's Lady Love by Alexa Aston
The Lyon's Laird by Hildie McQueen
The Lyon Sleeps Tonight by Elizabeth Ellen Carter
A Lyon in Her Bed by Amanda Mariel
Fall of the Lyon by Chasity Bowlin
Lyon's Prey by Anna St. Claire
Loved by the Lyon by Collette Cameron
The Lyon's Den in Winter by Whitney Blake
Kiss of the Lyon by Meara Platt
Always the Lyon Tamer by Emily E K Murdoch
To Tame the Lyon by Sky Purington
How to Steal a Lyon's Fortune by Alanna Lucas
The Lyon's Surprise by Meara Platt
A Lyon's Pride by Emily Royal
Lyon Eyes by Lynne Connolly
Tamed by the Lyon by Chasity Bowlin
Lyon Hearted by Jade Lee
The Devilish Lyon by Charlotte Wren
Lyon in the Rough by Meara Platt
Lady Luck and the Lyon by Chasity Bowlin
Rescued by the Lyon by C.H. Admirand
Pretty Little Lyon by Katherine Bone
The Courage of a Lyon by Linda Rae Sande
Pride of Lyons by Jenna Jaxon
The Lyon's Share by Cerise DeLand
The Heart of a Lyon by Anna St. Claire

Into the Lyon of Fire by Abigail Bridges
Lyon of the Highlands by Emily Royal
The Lyon's Puzzle by Sandra Sookoo
Lyon at the Altar by Lily Harlem
Captivated by the Lyon by C.H. Admirand
The Lyon's Secret by Laura Trentham
The Talons of a Lyon by Jude Knight
The Lyon and the Lamb by Elizabeth Keysian
To Claim a Lyon's Heart by Sherry Ewing

Chapter One

London, England
November 1818

Anyone watching might have assumed it was an ordinary card game, but Alexander Douglas, the sixth Earl of Wrotham, did not. It was Friday, and the day had waned, as had his attention. He'd consented to one more round of cards to allow his opponent the opportunity to win back some of his money after the man had pleaded. Predictably, the man continued to lose, and every hand dragged out into what seemed like an eternity. Anders's face became mottled, and his brow dripped with sweat. Alex almost felt sorry for him. Almost. As he waited for his opponent to lay down his last hand, a burst of cheers and shouts from a nearby table caught his attention.

Alex's lips twitched with suppressed humor. Someone had just given Lord Carl Markham a trouncing. Markham slammed his fist on the table, sending chips flying and toppling glasses. Alex moved to rise to lend help. Markham was a skillful player. He was also a bully and a brute. But the young man had kept his head. *Most impressive.* Alex didn't know the young man—at least, they didn't move in the same circles.

It wasn't the excessive stack of chips that earned his attention; it was the young man's odd appearance. *Peculiar chap.* The young man had thick brown muttonchop sideburns with a full mustache and yet looked scarcely old enough to be there. The young man turned, and Alex noted a mole tucked into the curve of his sideburn. He couldn't tell the actual shape, but it was noticeable enough from where Alex was sitting.

The den's floorman, Titan, stepped into the fray, leaning down to speak to Markham. Alex couldn't hear what Titan had said, but it was enough to make Markham get up and leave the table without further incident. Titan then turned to the young man and whispered something to him. The young man nodded. A moment later, the lad collected his winnings and got up from the table. The patrons cleared a path for him. Alex couldn't help but watch as the slender young man made his way through the den and left. *Curious indeed.*

A deep exhale from his opponent reminded Alex it was his turn. He surveyed the play and felt a mixture of sympathy and elation at being able to make his last hand. He wanted this game to end. As it was, he would own two letters from the man.

"Lord Anders, we played these last two games at your request," Alex returned, intentionally lowering his voice. "Perhaps another evening. I have a family engagement tonight and must be off."

The ashen-faced nobleman pushed away from the table. He withdrew a handkerchief from his waistcoat and patted his fevered brow to regain his bearings. A crowd had gathered around their table and had been steadily increasing, as had Earl Franklin Anders's desperate bets. "Well, my lord, I thank you for a most enlightening game," he said, scribbling a note and hastily signing his name. "I trust this will do for reparations."

The dim light and cigar smoke swirling about Alex's head made it hard to read the note. He squinted at the paper, moist with sweat that had barely allowed the ink to dry. "Yes, my lord. This is sufficient," he said, carefully tucking the letter in his waistcoat pocket alongside the other. "I'm making this my last hand, and I think the last trick belongs to me!" To punctuate his meaning, he turned the remaining card to display an ace of clubs.

Across from him, his opponent paled. "Wrotham, you must give me another chance to regain my losses."

Alex stood and caught the eye of his friend across the room. "It's time to go. I need to cash out my winnings and make it home in time to grab some food."

Mumbling something incoherent, the older gentleman pushed away from the table and stood with his handkerchief still in his hand. Turning, he ignored Alex's proffered hand and walked to the bar, most likely to grieve and nurse a bottle of whiskey.

"I can't blame you for leaving my game. This looked far more exciting," Alex said, approaching his friend, Viscount Sebastian Montgomery, who'd also been watching the Markham game.

Montgomery gave a brief nod as he sipped from the glass he held in his hand. "You missed a good show. Markham tried to cheat, and the young man bested him anyway."

"The widow keeps a tight rein on her tables. If she saw Markham cheating, his days of playing here may be limited. If they cheat the opponent, they will cheat the house. She's too savvy to allow someone of Markham's ilk to cause trouble because of cheating."

"The high-quality liquor she serves attracts the clientele." Montgomery paused. "What did you make of the young man that beat Markham? I heard his name was Mr. Paul Smith, but nothing more."

Alex hated going to the den. He hated gambling. But he was good at it and usually won. He never overplayed or overstayed, preferring to leave after a few hands, despite being a canny player. His late father had left the estate mired in debt—a shock, considering his family had been one of the wealthiest in the land. Gaming had never been a vice of his father's, but for reasons he couldn't fathom, his father had turned to gaming later in life. The late earl had been a terrible player whose spectacular losses had incurred such a mountain of debt that Alex had had no choice but to play to save his family's estate.

"Never heard of him. I'd say he bears watching." He could not deny an interest in the young man's talent.

Since his father's passing, Alex had been working tirelessly trying to untangle the web of lies, poor investments, and downright theft by his father's mistress. How could he not have known anything about what his father was doing? The late-life liaison with a manipulative mistress had been his father's undoing—and had nearly bankrupted his estate. The only alternative to gaming was proving the malicious influence one of London's most popular actresses had over his father's ailing mind. That was not an option Alex planned to pursue—at least not openly. It would be far too damaging for his mother and sister.

The actress, Delores Marble, had somehow recently gained a townhouse in Mayfair and was brazenly occupying the London property, flagrantly telling people his father had given it to her. Alex had made it his mission to restore the London townhouse property she had taken and repair the debts and his portfolio. He could do nothing about his father's reputation, as much as he wished he could. Tonight's winnings would ease many of the remaining balances. Even so, he had no appetite to bleed a fellow peer of his home, and it appeared Anders's pockets were empty—most likely from gaming.

"Will you feel up to billiards later tonight?" *That* was something he enjoyed.

"I'd be delighted… as long as you break out that reserve of French brandy you've been hiding," Montgomery agreed.

"Happy to. Mother will have dinner waiting when we get home. Afterward, I will challenge you to a game!" Alex intended to enjoy his time with Montgomery. Ever since his mother came out of mourning, she had demanded his attendance at the ridiculous gatherings his father had normally attended with her. Tomorrow, he had promised his mother he'd escort her and his younger sister, Louisa, to a small soiree, and failing to uphold that promise would make life difficult.

"So, what did you think of tonight's entertainment?" Montgomery asked.

"Quite the upset. Markham looked fit to be tied. I only wish I had watched the entire game and not just Markham's tantrum," Alex quipped. "Yes, I finished my game and watched most of it. Curious young fellow. Never seen him before. He looks strangely out of place, and yet I've seen no one play like that. Remarkable skill."

"Who is he? Perhaps he is a distant cousin to one of the *ton* families," his friend said as he passed his coat claim check to the woman staffing the coatroom.

"I noticed him, but I lost him when he stood to cash out his winnings," Alex said, accepting his coat. "I was trying to determine the best way to end the torturous game I was playing."

"Please don't make me feel sorry for you. If I had your talent, I would have had a hard time quitting."

"I know you, Montgomery. You have never been willing to take chances with your money, always turning your profit with more certain routes—hard work and investments. It would only take one loss before you would turn away from gambling."

"You are right there. You know me well."

"I do," Alex breathed. Montgomery was not only his best friend but almost like a brother to him. They had been through school and the war together—and both had served Wellington together in France following the war. It had only been a few months ago when the duke allowed some of the staff in France to return to England. Alex had been called home to take over the earldom at his father's death. Wellington had allowed both men to leave.

"We should make haste. Mother expects us for dinner. And do not weasel out of your promise to attend the Burleson soiree with me tomorrow night."

"I will keep my promise." Montgomery chortled. "Are you afraid marriage-minded mothers will attack you?"

"Something like that," Alex said, tossing his cane from his left to his right hand. "Mother will want to be there early. She refuses to be among the last arriving to any Burleson gathering—mostly because Lady Burleson always comments loudly with some sort of barely concealed snarly remark."

"Yet she continues to attend their events?" Montgomery pressed.

"I do not know why, but we're speaking about the illogical workings of women," Alex said, chuckling. Both men laughed at the jest until they opened the door to leave.

Icy rain driven by wind pelted their faces as Alex and his friend emerged from the light-blue-painted brick building on Cleveland Row. Across the street, he noticed two men in black overcoats come out of the stable and mount their horses. They both leaned into the wind and rode off toward town. "I'm glad we have a drier ride," he murmured to Montgomery as he held his hat in place and signaled his driver. A moment later, a sleek, black, unmarked coach pulled up to the curve. The driver made to jump down, but Alex halted him.

"We've got the door, Strafford. Stay where you are," Alex said, opening the door and hoisting himself onto the seat facing the back of the carriage. His friend jumped in and pulled the door closed.

"Where the hell did this storm come from?" grumbled Montgomery under his breath as he took the opposite seat, facing Alex. He removed his dripping hat and carefully tapped the water on the floor of the carriage. "Good man, your driver. A minute more in that deluge would have soaked us to the bone."

A moment later, the carriage lurched forward. The wind howled and rain pelted the windows. Alex was grateful to be dry.

"Indeed. We have Mother to thank for that. When it rains, they know to have the carriage waiting," he remarked as he adjusted himself and rested his cane beside him.

"You have a flair for cards, Wrotham. I noticed you had the attention of the entire room—until the young lad with the bushy sideburns beat Markham. Be careful, old friend. This is the fifth win you've had there this month. You've surely landed in her sights with that cleanup tonight," Montgomery commented as the carriage jolted forward, rolling over the cobblestones on the sparsely lit road.

"You're referring to the Black Widow?" Alex replied, more of a statement than a question. He shuddered inwardly. That was the last person he wanted the attention of.

Montgomery snorted. "You were generous to stop playing when you did. Anders seemed determined to keep playing, despite his rotten luck."

"Admittedly, I've had a lucky run, but I don't enjoy pounding a man when he's down. I know when it's time to hold. These winnings cover my father's remaining debts and leave me enough for some investments we discussed."

"Only if you don't lose them. The widow doesn't like the house to lose. She keeps a sharp tab on everyone that enters the Lyon's Den. If you continue to gamble there, you may find yourself in worse shape than when you inherited," his friend persisted.

"You are referring to her penchant for snaring many of her upstanding guests in the parson's noose—especially those who overindulge in her expensive liquors." Alex had resolved not to drink more than one per visit. So far, he had held to that standard. "You make a good point. I should take my winnings and count myself fortunate."

Montgomery nodded. "I know life was simpler before."

"You mean my investments and the connections…" Alex didn't bother to finish his sentence.

"I know that look. You plan to continue?" Montgomery pressed, his tone incredulous.

"I have little choice. The debts have been paid, but the townhouse in Mayfair is in Marble's possession. Frankly, I'm surprised Mother hasn't mentioned it. And unfortunately, I'm still in no position to confront her, and I have yet to find the proof that she hoodwinked Father out of it." His mother made no mention of her husband's liaison with the actress, adding to Alex's hope that no one had mentioned his late father's activities. Alex's solicitors were looking into Mrs. Marble's claims to the London property in Mayfair.

"Have you heard from the woman since refusing her offer to continue your father's liaison?"

"Not yet. My younger brother Thomas has connections to the head of the Bow Street Runners, and they are looking into her background."

"So, Thomas knows the extent of the debt?"

"He does. I thought it prudent that he should be aware of all that I know. The woman is relentless. When I refused Marble's offer, she vowed it wasn't the end of our 'association.'"

"That fits with what I've heard of her. She doesn't handle rejection well," Montgomery said. "She's also reputed to be connected to the underworld. Sleep with one eye open."

Alex tapped his cane.

Montgomery gave a hearty laugh. "Perhaps I don't need to worry as much. Most people might think you use the cane to support a leg injury. They could be very surprised to find themselves facing a master swordsman at the end of your rapier."

Alex smiled. "You make a good point about the company she keeps, so I will remain alert. She's a shifty one. I'm still not convinced Father gifted her that townhouse, but I must find proof." The very thought of the woman riled his temper. He couldn't recall a person who made him angrier.

"I'm sure with our work and connections with the Home Office, they would help. Have you given thought to asking for help with this?"

"I had hoped to solve it myself, but if she is connected to other nefarious players, I'd best know all that I can. I'll meet with Lord Kitterman at the Home Office. You're like a brother to me. Without you, they might have tempted me to further chance my good fortune tonight." Alex patted his chest, where he had secured his winnings in a special interior pocket and leaned on his cane. "I need a better plan—one that involves less chance and less alcohol," he added wryly as he glanced out the window at the darkening sky.

"Before I stepped away to watch the young lad in the mutton-chops, you had won several thousand pounds, and you also hold two letters from Anders. That's a small fortune," Montgomery asserted.

Alex nudged open the curtain and glanced out of the window. Usually, an occasional gaslight stood on corners of the street, but it was eerily dark, and he wondered if the gaslights had blown out or been turned off. "Did you pack a sidearm?"

"Yes," Montgomery said, patting his pocket, "but I'm hoping to exercise my right arm serving up a well-earned scotch once we arrive at your house."

The hair prickled on the back of Alex's neck. "I'm not sure you will get your wish. Something feels off. Did you notice the two men dressed in black who left the stables on horseback when Strafford pulled up with the carriage?"

"Yes, you remarked something about being glad our ride home was dry."

The surface of the street changed beneath the wheels of the carriage from cobblestones to gravel. They had rounded a corner and were away from the busier part of Cleveland Row, into an isolated section of the road. It usually took a few minutes to rejoin the busier and better-lit part of town.

The sound of hooves racing alongside the carriage had both men drawing their weapons: Alex his cane, and Montgomery his pistol.

Alex twisted the end of the cane, pulled out the rapier, and drew his gun. They heard Strafford's shout just moments before the carriage made a sharp right turn, throwing both men against the door as it rolled on two wheels, before finally righting itself.

"Thieves! We're being attacked, my lord," Strafford shouted, then cursed.

The carriage pitched forward, listed for a moment, and then came to an abrupt stop.

"Ready, old friend?" Alex asked Montgomery.

"Always, old friend."

Alex and Montgomery exited from opposite sides of the carriage just as Strafford yelled, "Off with ye, you blackguards, or I'll send you both to hell with holes in your chest!" The air split with the loud *boom* of the driver's blunderbuss fire, followed by the return of pistol fire. A highwayman leaped from the top of the carriage as a body slumped forward. Without needing to check, Alex knew Strafford had taken a bullet. *Blast! I can't assist Strafford until I secure these brigands.*

A darkly clad man uttered an obscenity as he scrambled from the bramble brush near the side of the road.

"Ah! There you are." Before Alex could be upon him, the man stood and withdrew a large knife. "I'll be relieving you of that generous payday ye 'ad back at the Lyon's Den, milord," he said in a low, menacing tone.

Alex glanced at the top of the carriage but saw no signs of Strafford moving. Fury filled him. "Nay!" he returned, his tone deadly. "I will do the *taking*. Your partner shot my driver and signed your death warrant," Alex seethed as he prepared to fight.

"Ye're one of 'em *pretty* lords. That's too bad, because I don't fight fair," the bandit sneered, lunging at Alex with a blade that appeared a foot long.

Alex arched back and stepped aside, deftly avoiding the knife. Before the man could react, Alex thrust his sword. "You should watch the deadly end of my sword and not admire my face," he said, slicing through the sleeve of the bandit's knife-wielding arm. Blood erupted in a spray. "You seem to be bleeding profusely there," he taunted the bandit in a lethal voice. "Drop to your knees, or I'll finish you."

The man complied, dropping his knife and falling to his knees in front of Alex.

"Not so fast, guvnor," a nasal voice said, as a shorter man dressed in black, with a black mask that covered most of his face, stepped from behind the carriage wielding a pistol. "I've not fired my gun, and at this distance, you make an easy target."

"As are you," Montgomery said from the darkness behind the thief. "I assure you, my gun is loaded, and as you can tell, it's pressed against your back. As my friend just said… on your knees… *now!*"

He prodded the stocky man holding the gun with the barrel of his own gun and sent a questioning look in Alex's direction, at the man's friend, already on his knees. The short man cursed and also got down on his knees.

"I'll take this." Montgomery snatched the man's gun and pocketed it before binding the man's hands behind him.

Alex finished binding the taller man's hands and then fished in the robber's jacket, withdrawing a small pouch of coins that he recognized as Strafford's. "Pounds sterling," he mused aloud. "These appear to be my driver's, so I'll relieve you of that burden." It was the least he could do for Strafford.

The driver, who'd sat slumped in his seat, let out a groan.

"How do you fare, Strafford?"

"I'm alive, milord. But that's all I can swear to," Strafford croaked.

He sounded bad, but Alex sent a small petition above, asking God to keep him alive; Alex still needed to get him to a physician. He pocketed the coins and jerked the bandit up from the ground.

"Leave it! That's me money! She told me whatever we took, it—" The man stopped speaking and glared. "You'll pay for this, Wrotham," he ground out just as Alex shoved a rag in the taller man's mouth.

"*She?* And there's the matter of *my name* on your lips. You've piqued my curiosity," Alex said, shoving him in the carriage next to his partner, who sat bound and gagged. "That's quite an ambitious threat you're issuing from your position." With the blade of his rapier, Alex leaned in and sliced through the binds of their masks to reveal their faces.

Alex routinely noted his surroundings—a habit he had honed while working with the intelligence service. He didn't recognize the taller one but recalled having glimpsed the shorter one with Anders earlier that *day*. And he also recalled having seen him another time.

"Do you two work for Lord Anders?" It was more of a statement than a question. He already knew the answer. "You," he said to the shorter one. "I noticed you helping Lady Anders in town last week. You drew my notice when you dropped her boxes and she screamed at you. I believe she had just left the modiste." He leaned closer until his breath almost touched the bandit's face. "Anders lost quite a bit today. Did he ask you to follow us?"

Silence.

"I already know the answer, and the man will regret that decision." Incensed, he continued, "You also mentioned a 'she.' To whom did you refer? Be very careful… you want to be very certain of what you say." With his rapier, he touched the man's chin and drew a small stream of blood.

Both men remained quiet.

Montgomery opened the other door. "I'll drive." Then he added in a low voice, "Strafford has a wound on his side. I've bound it, but he's lost a lot of blood."

"We need to get these bastards to the magistrate," Alex fumed. "And I'll pay a visit to the Black Widow. Her men might be interested to know what these two have been up to with Anders."

As the carriage lurched forward, Alex watched the two men sitting across from him—both bound and gagged. Anders had targeted him before their game concluded at the Lyon's Den. That much was obvious, but how would they know he had winnings? He could have been a big loser. He had a nagging feeling he had seen the other one before, too, but couldn't recall where.

No matter. He'd be working on this until he had answers. Tomorrow night, he would play the dutiful son and escort his mother and younger sister to the Burleson soiree.

Chapter Two

The next day

Lady Priscilla Giffard smoothed her skirt and checked her reflection in the looking glass.

"You look lovely, my lady," her abigail said, securing the pearl earrings before stepping back. "They are lovely with the curls framing your face."

"Thank you, Mary," Lady Priscilla replied. She stared at the orange satin evening dress she wore and wrinkled her brow. Orange had become the bane of her existence ever since her first pianoforte recital. The color was one of her mother's favorites, and she had decided it would be Priscilla's color. Lady Burleson felt especially partial to bright pinks, oranges, and lime green. There was a reason no one else in the *ton* gravitated to those colors. They did nothing for you unless you were a fish in a pond.

A giggle escaped her as she imagined pink and lime green koi in her mother's garden pond. It would certainly give the barn cats more amusement.

Earlier in the day, Priscilla had scanned the ballroom for her usual hiding places. But for this gathering, Lady Burleson had ordered the decorator to remove the potted plants that had always provided cover. *Daughter, you must put yourself out there. There is someone for everyone,* her mother had insisted. It was what Mama always said, and so far, she had been wrong.

There had been no pursuits by young men—no courting, and especially no dancing. Not even so much as a glass of lemonade offered to quench Priscilla's thirst. And if this soiree followed the path of the others before it, there would be no dances. Life had seemed hopeless—until she had developed her plan. Once she turned twenty-one, she would be firmly on the shelf, and Mama would forget about her. If she made enough money, perhaps she could purchase a small house or take a job as a companion. Priscilla wasn't sure how much she'd need and hadn't given thought too much beyond earning the money. But there would be time for planning later.

Tonight would be a repeat of all the other social events they had forced her to attend, and she needed to steel herself for what was to come. Priscilla would spend the evening with the wallflowers. No surprise there. If she had escaped the notice of any young man in the *ton*, their parents could apprise them of their oversight. Nearly everyone in the *ton* was familiar with the Burleson musicales.

Those horrible musicales. She hated them. Her mother forced Priscilla and her sister, Jane, to perform in front of the *ton*; Priscilla sang while her sister accompanied her on the pianoforte. Priscilla knew she had no voice for singing—a knowledge confirmed by the endless looks of pain on the forced attendees' faces. And Jane could barely play the pianoforte. Priscilla had heard all the whispers. *Those girls have no talent.*

She snorted at the thought. No disagreement there. Yet if her mother invited them, they attended—unless something else... *like death...* excused them from the performance. No one dared to miss a Burleson event. Her mother was a woman with a long memory who wasn't timid about using her ample influence. So... everyone suffered.

Priscilla's younger sister, Rose, had no idea what was in store for her at ten years. *I hope with all my heart that Rose has true talent and likes bright colors.*

For Priscilla, the dreadful ordeals characterized her mother's endless control of her life. She longed for freedom more than anything and saw spinsterhood as her only chance for that.

Enduring humiliation and the stutter it caused her had become the norm, especially since her entrance into Society. She was cursed with thick, wavy red hair and pale skin, and her oval face held nothing spectacular… unless you counted the lavender eyes she had inherited from her grandmother.

But no one remarked on her eyes because no one saw them. Her mother deemed orange to be her best color, and so every dress had a bright orange as its central hue. Even printed cloth was predominantly orange. The dreadful color reflected in her eyes and turned them a muddy brown, as did the yellow and lime green. All three colors made her appear sallow, and she was often questioned by well-intentioned ladies as to whether she felt well. Despite all her efforts, and those of the modiste, Madame Soyeuse, Mama had refused Priscilla's preferences and insisted on picking fabrics for both girls' wardrobes.

Priscilla consistently chose deep greens, navy, russet, and burgundy cloth—colors that she thought enhanced her coloring—and Madame Soyeuse agreed. It mattered not. Her mother always changed them to this hideous orange. Priscilla shuddered. She felt like a peacock—an orange one—from her satin shoes to the jeweled feather in her auburn red hair.

Mama insisted the colors projected her daughters to the *ton*. *Like fireworks,* Priscilla thought sardonically. Forced notoriety humiliated her; she much preferred obscurity. Her stutter, which occurred when she felt objectified or humiliated, made things worse. Then there were the mean whispers.

Her hands twisted in pain and frustration.

Jane had lovely almond eyes, bow-shaped lips, and dark brown hair. She was a younger version of her mother, who had been quite a beauty in her day. Practically every color flattered her—or at least didn't disparage her attributes. She could wear anything Mama required. The musicales had done Jane no favors, but they hadn't hurt her as much as they had Priscilla.

"Mary, by any chance, have you pressed the deep olive dress Madame Soyeuse added to my last order?"

"The one you added after your mama left the store with Jane?" Mary asked hesitantly. "She delivered it separately, to me, fearing your mother's reaction. It is behind your other dresses in the closet."

"I'm truly sorry to have put you and Madame Soyeuse in such an awkward position, but I fear there are so few options."

Priscilla dropped her cup of chocolate to the floor, watching as the dark liquid covered the bottom of her hated dress. She swallowed and bit her bottom lip, willing the pain to squelch any outward display of her satisfaction.

"I apologize for my clumsiness, Mary. It appears this dress has gotten into a bit of trouble. I will need a quick change." She looked up at Mary and noticed the maid was also biting her lower lip, and looking away, clearly struggling not to laugh.

"Oh! My lady, I fear your dress is ruined. There is no way I can remove all the chocolate—not before the dance," the maid said slowly. "Your olive-green dress is in the back of the wardrobe, as you asked. The guests will arrive soon, so I don't believe any other alternative exists."

"Help me dress," Priscilla said, standing. "Mother will not be pleased, but I shall handle it. I gave you no choice."

Ten minutes later, Priscilla checked her reflection. This time, she felt more at ease. Surely Mama would not make a big thing of it with the guests arriving. "Oh, wait. We need to remove this hideous feather in my hair. Can you add these combs?" Priscilla sat down to allow

Mary to make the change.

"These are lovely, my lady. Are they new?" Mary asked as she removed the feather and inserted the combs. "I have never seen such lovely silver combs. The emeralds and diamonds are exquisite."

"My grandmother gave them to me. She told me to put them away until I had a special dress to wear with them. I'm sure she will recognize them when she sees them tonight."

"Oh! That's right! The Dowager Countess Burleson will be in attendance. I heard the cook say she had made one of her favorite desserts. Your grandmother is a beautiful woman. Most kind."

"I was thrilled to hear she had returned from her trip. She has my red hair and complexion, and a better appreciation of what apparel would complement my coloring," Priscilla said, touching the beautifully adorned combs. "I think I'm ready."

"Your shoes!" Mary pointed out.

Priscilla laughed. "Oh goodness! You're quite right! I can't wear these. There should be some that will match at the back of the wardrobe. Check the small brown bag."

She would have sworn she heard Mary giggle. But she said nothing. The maid retrieved the shoes and stepped back. "That color matches perfectly, Lady Priscilla. It suits you." She waited a moment. "Will there be anything else?"

"If I could delay it any longer, I would," Priscilla said with a sigh. "I suppose it's time."

"Yes, my lady. Your mother expects you and your sister to assist with greeting the guests. You must hurry," her maid said as she tidied up the vanity.

"It's most unusual. Normally, she and Papa greet the guests. Has Jane gone downstairs?"

"Yes, my lady. She joined your parents a few minutes ago."

Heavens! Jane was downstairs, so Priscilla was already late. There was nothing else she could do but join her family and face the firing squad. Her mother would not be pleased.

"I'll be right behind you, Mary." Pinching her cheeks, Priscilla took a lingering look in the looking glass, unable to resist the sensation of smug satisfaction from wearing her green dress. She smiled at her reflection, then hurried out of her room and closed the door behind her.

Mary had done wonders taming her normally unruly hair, she thought as she raced downstairs to face her mother. Gently, she touched the soft curls that framed her face and smiled, pleased with the style and the silky feel.

"Darling, our guests are arriving," her mother said without turning around, as Priscilla entered the room. "Be a love and stand next to your sister to help us welcome them."

At least she isn't demanding we perform on the pianoforte tonight, Priscilla thought, feeling thankful. She could hear the orchestra playing in the ballroom.

"The Earl and Countess of Egerton," their butler, Arlington, announced, as the handsome couple worked their way through the Giffards' short receiving line. Priscilla smiled as her mother's eyes followed the countess as she moved past. But seeing her daughter provoked an audible gasp.

"You look lovely, Priscilla," Jane whispered, squeezing her sister's hand.

"Viscount Southwood and Viscountess Southwood," Arlington continued, announcing the Countess of Egerton's parents.

"Phoebe, it is good to see you," Lady Burleson sputtered. "I... was just noticing how your lovely daughter has become—even more beautiful since marriage."

"Thank you, Henrietta. That is generous of you," Lady Southwood said, squeezing her friend's hand. She nodded toward Priscilla and Jane. "Your daughters look exceptionally lovely tonight. Jane looks fetching in that lovely pink confection, and I simply adore the beautiful green silk Priscilla is wearing. Quite attractive on her. It brings out the beautiful color of her eyes." She moved closer to Priscilla, giving her a tender smile. "I don't believe I had ever noticed your lavender eyes, my dear. Simply stunning."

Mama turned in Priscilla's direction and forced a smile. "Yes, the color has been a surprise," she replied pleasantly between clenched teeth—still smiling and giving polite nods to her guests as they filed past. "I had never considered it until very recently."

"With that hair and those eyes, she looks like perfection," Lady Southwood said, before patting her husband's arm—most likely a signal she was ready to continue into the ballroom.

When a break occurred in the queue of their guests, Priscilla's father stepped over to her. "The color becomes you, my dear," he said, looking meaningfully in his wife's direction, before kissing each of his daughters' cheeks.

An audible huff of breath caused Priscilla to look at her mother and see the eyeroll. Her signature mannerism.

"Mama, it's a dress," Priscilla said, stretching out the last syllable in frustration. "Would you rather I wore the orange one with chocolate stains on the bottom? Besides, this dress seems to have gotten me quite noticed. Isn't that the object of these affairs?"

Judging from the arched eyebrows, Priscilla judged she had gone a hair too far.

"We will discuss this later," her mother said through gritted teeth and a forced smile.

"Certainly, Mama," Priscilla said in a subdued tone, quashing a surging feeling of elation. Her father liked the dress. However, she knew he would not agree with her methods if he found out what she had done. While it was wrong to disobey her mother's edicts, Mama refused to consider her feelings—even when the modiste pointed to colors that would flatter her. According to her mother, Priscilla needed to marry, so she would not be in the way of her sister's success.

Perhaps it was the money she had been earning, although *earning* seemed the wrong word to use for her recent activity. They were winnings. Yet winning the money had felt *freeing*.

And having a fashionable alternative to the hideous frock her mother wanted her to wear had been delicious. The idea to ruin the frothy orange one had been without forethought and born of frustration, and the notion had taken root moments before she had emptied her cup onto it. Her most pressing concern was keeping Mary free of her mother's recriminations. She had done this, not her abigail, and meant to protect her. Mary didn't agree with her gambling and certainly didn't approve of her going to Cleveland Row, but she understood Priscilla and agreed to keep her secret and help with the disguise.

Priscilla's first rule was the one her father had preached when he had taught her to play cards years ago. *Never bet more than you have in your pocket to lose—in case you lose.* So far, she had adhered to it rigidly. Her second rule was to keep her ruse tightly under wraps.

A footman came by with a tray of champagne. There was a break in the guest line. Glancing in her mother's direction, and seeing her in a discussion with the butler, Priscilla accepted a glass, taking a restorative gulp before quickly placing the drink on a hall table behind her. *I need all the fortitude I can muster.*

"Priscilla..." her mother began in her shrill voice.

"Wife... give it a rest. It's a dress," her father cut in, huffing in frustration. He rarely went against his wife's dictates but seemed unmoved by her red-faced anger. "I think the green a pleasant color for her," he added in a voice that brooked no argument.

Mama glared at the earl but said nothing. Priscilla had never known her father to step in between her and her mother, and she was unfamiliar with the feeling the satisfaction his vindication lent her. But he had witnessed her mother's tantrum, and she was grateful for the reprieve.

She relaxed and thought about her triumphant engagement at the Lyon's Den the afternoon before. But it wasn't the money she thought about. It was the deliciously handsome man who had been sitting two tables away—the one who, when he had smiled, created a distraction that nearly cost her the game. Luckily, she had reviewed her cards a second time before making her move.

Having endured three Seasons and not attracting any suitors, Priscilla had no illusions of making a match. Her parents were very wealthy, but unless she was content to become someone's companion, she needed to put away enough money to support herself. She knew she would end up as a spinster, but had no plans to remain at home with an overbearing mother.

Aside from her lady's maid, the only person familiar with her afternoon disguise was Mrs. Bessie Dove-Lyon, the widow of her father's former best friend, and the proprietress of the Lyon's Den, a well-known gambling house on Cleveland Row.

Priscilla possessed no talent a potential husband might deem worthy. Her talent began and ended with dancing, despite Mama's best efforts. She had taken the lessons in comportment and dancing seriously but despised needlepoint and painting. However, she was extremely talented at card games—and grateful to her father for teaching her. When she'd shown an uncanny talent for cards, he quietly furthered her instruction whenever they found time. Priscilla enjoyed playing cards, particularly whist, hearts, and piquet.

Priscilla had been mulling over the idea of using her only talent as a way out of the hopeless humiliation in which her mother kept her shackled when she ran into the woman at the local milliner's. Biting her lower lip, Priscilla steeled herself as she approached her father's best friend's widow. "M-m-might I visit you on the morrow, M-Mrs. Dove-Lyon?" she asked. *Oh God! Why couldn't she speak without stuttering? It happened every time she became overset or anxious.*

"I will be glad to entertain you, my lady! Will the countess be joining us?" the widow inquired.

"No, Mrs. Dove-Lyon. My abigail will accompany me."

The woman gave a slight nod. "And your father... does he still enjoy good health?"

"He does, Mrs. Dove-Lyon."

"That is good. Well then, shall I expect you tomorrow?" the widow asked.

"I will do my best to be there tomorrow," Priscilla heard herself say.

The next day, she feigned a headache when her mother asked her to accompany her on a call to a grieving widow. As soon as her mother and sister left, Priscilla dressed and, with her maid, took a hack to Cleveland Row. She had seized on the opportunity to take her life into her own hands.

"The Earl of Wrotham, the Countess of Wrotham, and Viscount Sebastian Montgomery." Arlington's stentorian voice penetrated her thoughts.

Priscilla blinked before looking into the silver-gray eyes of the earl. Russet-brown hair dipped in a wave over the man's right eye, and the length of his hair slightly touched his collar.

Priscilla caught her breath as he picked up her gloved hand. He was the man she had seen two tables away at the Lyon's Den. The blood drained from her face and, placing a gloved hand behind her on the table holding her champagne flute, she struggled not to faint. A sideways glance at her mother showed her wearing a pleased, expectant smile.

"My lord," her mother said in her usual taut voice. "Allow me to introduce my daughter, Lady Priscilla."

Chapter Three

Alex took a half step back, unprepared for the beauty that stood in front of him. Her perfectly coiffured red hair framed a delicate oval face with generous lips. A sumptuous green silk dress with a delicate overlay of diamond-studded chiffon clung to a slender, perfectly shaped figure. She was one of the most beautiful women he had ever seen. Slightly taller than most Society misses, she easily reached his chin, but it was her sparkling lavender eyes that drew his attention most of all. This divine goddess could not be the same many in the *ton* claimed had assaulted their ears. *Surely not.*

"It is my pleasure, Lady Priscilla," he said, suddenly remembering himself. He leaned in and reached for her gloved right hand, only to find it buried in the folds of her satin dress. Deftly, the woman withdrew her left hand, causing the corners of his mouth to twitch in amusement. Unwilling to draw undue attention, he picked it up and lightly kissed it. An alluring scent of vanilla and bergamot stirred his senses and drew his attention again to the lovely red curls framing her face. He had never seen such beautiful eyes. "I cannot recall us meeting before, but I have the uncanny feeling we have." His voice was low.

"I-I don't believe so, my lord," she stammered. "I cannot recall ever being formally introduced."

The sound of the orchestra warming up with a reel sounded in the distance. "Do you have your dance card, my lady?"

"Yes, my lord," Lady Priscilla said, extending it to him.

He took the proffered pencil and signed his name. "I have claimed the first waltz," he said smoothly.

"I look forward to it, my lord," she replied with a slight dip.

Alex looked over his shoulder and noticed that Montgomery had also taken note of the slender beauty.

"Lady Priscilla, it is my pleasure," his friend said, giving a slight bow before following Alex inside. "She seems familiar," Montgomery whispered to Alex as they entered the room. "But I must ask, what was that all about with the glove? Do you think she is missing a hand?"

Alex snorted. "It was strange. Perhaps her hand is scarred. Yet I recall she used both hands to greet my mother. But you are right: I had a similar sensation we had met before but cannot place her. I mentioned it, but she insisted *not*. Perhaps she is right. I know without question I'd recall those eyes and that glorious red hair." He turned around and watched his mother make her way over after speaking to some friends that had entered behind them.

"My dears," she said with a wide smile, finally catching up with them. "I've volunteered you both to dance with Lady Albertine's twin daughters, Lady Alice, and Lady Esther. I assured Lady Albertine that once they danced with you and Lord Montgomery, other partners would follow. I will be happy to provide an introduction." She looked in the direction of a cluster of mothers and daughters, but didn't see them, and waved her hand in dismissal. "And, of course, you should dance with one of Lady Burleson's daughters. It is the polite thing to do."

"Mother." He bit his tongue, struggling against a burst of irritation. She never failed to attempt some level of matchmaking with a young lady meeting her approval. At least she was consistent, he mused. However, it would not work.

"I doubt that will be an issue," Montgomery said in a playful tone.

"Stubble it, Montgomery," Alex whispered, before attempting to salve the conversation with his mother. "I have already promised to dance with Lady Priscilla, and I will—"

"For the entire event?" his mother asked, in a slightly sharp tone.

Lady Burleson and his mother had never had what he would term a cordial relationship, but still, her reaction startled him. Did his mother not approve of Lady Priscilla? "No, of course not, but after these dances you have graciously *assigned me*, I plan to join the other men," he said slowly.

"In the game room." She tutted disapprovingly. "I don't ask much of you, son. And I had hoped your accepting to escort me would mean more than the usual one or two dances before you disappear." She heaved a sigh. "I've never known you to gamble so much, son, and I'm not at all comfortable with it."

"Mother," he said, biting back a note of censure with a slow exhalation of breath. Rarely did he find himself so immediately annoyed with her. "Quite right, Mother. A peer of our status dancing with the young ladies does improve their dance cards."

Saying that aloud made him feel a little guilty. Once an earl danced with a young lady, others would follow suit. However, surveying the room of delicate, hopeful debutantes awash in pastels and pasted smiles hastened his need to escape to the cardroom.

"I want Louisa to be successful, but I'm in no mood to sacrifice myself on the altar of hopeful debutantes. I will mingle and make a charitable showing among the ladies, but I feel no need to defend my desire to play cards."

He caught his mother's glare before she replaced it with a look of nonchalance. "Please forgive me. I should not have obligated you or Lord Montgomery, and I should not have been so sharp in my response. I find myself with such handsome men accompanying me, and my attention is more in demand than usual," she said in a light tone. "Lady Albertine stopped me and—"

"We never mind dancing with lovely women," Montgomery intervened.

Leave it to Montgomery to soften the situation, even when she inserted him in her machinations.

Curiously, he found himself looking forward to playing cards. Social events gave him easy and practical insight into other players' skills.

The band struck a loud note, signaling the dancing would begin. In a moment, the chords of a familiar waltz filled the room, and he searched for the red-haired beauty in dark green, rustling silk. *Ah, there she is,* he thought, watching her accept a flute of champagne before taking a seat with the wallflowers. "I've promised the first dance," he said, giving a brief bow to his mother.

He wove his way in Lady Priscilla's direction until he stood in front of her.

Smiling, he gave a gallant bow before extending his arm. "I believe this is our dance, my lady."

Startled, she looked up. "Y-yes, my lord," she said, placing her flute on a small table beside the chair. She gave a quick look at her sister, who offered a nod of encouragement. "I would be delighted, my lord," she said, seeming a little more confident as she accepted his proffered arm. But then her voice dropped to a conspiratorial whisper. "Are you sure you want it to be a waltz? You would be my first waltz partner."

"I'll hold your seat for you, Priscilla," Jane interjected, encouraging her sister with a smile.

Her first waltz? How can that be? A wry smile quirked his mouth. "Then the men of the *ton* are blind. It'll be my pleasure to be your first waltz partner," he said.

Hearing male footsteps behind him, Alex turned. It was Montgomery, who had followed him.

"If I promise to leave your toes intact, would you consent to this dance with me, my lady?" his friend asked Lady Jane.

"The color green becomes you, my lady," Alex offered as he and Priscilla took their places on the dance floor and began to waltz. "I don't believe you have never done this," he said as he turned her gently.

"Thank you, my lord," she replied.

Her voice held an uncommon throatiness that sounded almost seductive, stimulating a sensory reaction that ran the length of him. Her eyes lifted to meet his, and he held them. "I apologize for not allowing you to enjoy your champagne. It was my good fortune to find you still seated but in a most unlikely area."

She laughed softly. "If you mean with the wallflowers, you flatter me, my lord. Many of my closest friendships have formed along those walls during my parents' parties."

He let his gaze wander over the petite beauty in his arms—as her words reminded him of something his sister had said that morning.

Lady Burleson's daughters usually wear such pained expressions at their mother's events. It's difficult to feign excitement when the patroness's own family dreads them.

Priscilla's countenance held no dread. Quite the opposite, she seemed absorbed in the movements.

"I'm not sure what to make of that commentary, but you do not belong among the wallflowers."

For a moment, she remained quiet as they whirled to the music. Then she broke her silence. "I don't recall you attending my mother's… events. I would have noticed… you as often as my sister and I faced the audience."

A blush crept up her neck, and he felt her tense. "I would have remembered meeting you, as well," he offered, hoping to soothe her disquiet.

Of course! He had heard of the *infamous Burleson musicales*, as his mother referred to them. Somehow, he had managed to be away when they occurred, or when he had been home, his father had escorted his sister and mother.

"I left the country for a few years," he explained. Technically, he *had* been out of the country working intelligence for England—something he hoped to continue.

"Oh, that would explain it." She visibly brightened, and her slightly husky voice seemed lighter.

Something intrigued him about this young woman—besides her voice. They stepped back, and he moved her into a gentle spin. "I believe you undersell your waltzing experience, my lady," he said as they stepped back together.

A coy smile stole onto her face. "Perhaps it is your ability to lead, my lord."

The song ended, and they stopped for a moment, staring at one another before he extended his arm to return her to the wallflowers' section. "You should not hide in this corner, Lady Priscilla. It would honor me if you can save me another waltz." The words were out before he could think about them. While he could not deny he had enjoyed their dance, he was usually one and done.

She flicked the dance card hanging from her wrist, but he noticed she didn't remove it. "I'm sure there will be plenty of dances," she said, glancing up.

It was as if she thought no one would dance with her. Her eyes were striking, but there was something more about her.

He cleared his throat as two young men came up from behind him and asked if they could sign her dance card, which she extended.

Catching the look on his face, she placed the card in Alex's outstretched palm. He scribbled his name and passed it to the gentleman on his left, who quickly scribbled his and looked up at Alex, who was still standing there.

"I will be back after this next dance, my lady," the young man said.

She nodded. "Thank you. I will look forward to it."

"I find I could use something to quench my thirst. Would you care for some lemonade?" Alex heard himself ask. He had fulfilled his obligation to dance with her, yet he seemed to find reasons to come back. He had asked for a second dance… and now, lemonade. *What am I thinking?*

He was thinking, he reminded himself, that she was the most beautiful woman he had seen in an age. And he wanted to spend more time with her.

Her eyes held a puzzled look. "I would, my lord."

Montgomery returned with Lady Jane at that moment.

"Priscilla, Grandmama has arrived!" Jane gushed, turning heads as the Dowager Countess Burleson entered the room. She seemed to spot her granddaughters immediately and headed their way.

"I should get the lemonade," Alex said.

"I see Lord Stephens entering, and I would like to have a word," Montgomery said. "I'll find you in a few minutes."

Alex nodded. Approaching the refreshment tables, he noticed his mother off to the side, speaking to one of her friends. Lady Albertine, if he wasn't mistaken. They were standing with their backs to him. *Good.* If he worked this out right, he could snare two glasses of lemonade and be off before they noticed him.

Deliberately, he walked to the opposite end of the table, where a second urn of lemonade sat. With both glasses in hand, he turned to go, but hearing Lady Priscilla's name bantered in a most unseemly manner drew his attention, and he stepped closer.

"It was most kind of your son and his friend to dance with the elder Burleson girl," Lady Albertine said with a sniff. "She was probably foisted upon him when Henrietta had a chance to set her hooks in him—after all, they are nobility."

"You speak of my son, Janet," his mother said. He smiled, thinking of how she would have drawn herself up to her full height. She might, or might not, like someone for personal reasons, but he'd never known her to tolerate such maliciousness.

"I apologize, my dear. It's just that everyone knows what they will be left with if they become entangled with those young women. No talent, and no awareness they lack it. Most assuredly, once he dances with my Alice, the Burleson girl will take her place with the others who are unable to compete."

"Mabel, we have been acquaintances a long time, but I don't believe I ever realized how much of a snob you are, and I am sorry I asked my son and his friend to do you a kindness. I am certain Alex and Lord Montgomery will dance with your daughters, but it will be because I asked him to do it."

"How insulting!" Lady Albertine exclaimed.

"Indeed!" his mother replied curtly before he heard the furious rustling of skirts.

He knew his mother not to engage in malicious gossip but was incredulous at having heard her censure the condescending Lady Albertine—the woman was someone to be avoided. *Odious woman,* he thought.

Leaving in the opposite direction, he moved quickly before he was noticed. This event was becoming more interesting by the minute.

"Wrotham."

Relieved, he turned. "Montgomery."

"I'm feeling rather beset by the marriage-minded mamas, and I have no wish to be entrapped. Once I've complied with your mother's request, I will meet you in the game room. I'll save you a chair." Montgomery looked at the glasses of lemonade in Alex's hands and grinned. "Have you changed your drink of choice?"

Alex sighed and lifted the glasses in mock defeat. "I'm not sure what I've done tonight. But no, I haven't changed my drink. Your plan sounds solid. I shall join you, soon."

He quickly scanned the room and spotted Lady Priscilla speaking to a young lord. His mother's conversation with Lady Albertine had firmed up his plans, and he walked briskly in Lady Priscilla's direction, approaching from behind her. "Your lemonade, my lady."

"Th-thank you, your lordship," she said, accepting the glass.

"Miss Priscilla, I look forward to our dance." The young man standing next to her glanced up. "Lord Harrison," Alex acknowledged him.

"Lord Wrotham," the younger man said, giving a polite nod before excusing himself.

As the band struck up a waltz, Alex set down his glass. "I believe this is our dance, my lady."

"Are you certain you wish another waltz?" she asked tentatively. "My lord, you were under no obligation to dance with me a second time."

"I am certain." Captivated by the pair of sparkling lavender eyes looking up at him, he bowed over her outstretched, and gloved, hand before leading her over to their places on the dance floor.

Alex glanced to his right and saw his mother speaking to another one of her friends. As he whirled past, he saw his mother give a fleeting nod, before he returned his attention to the beautiful woman in his arms. Undoubtedly, Lady Burleson had a reputation as heavy-handed in her approach to launching her daughters in Society, using the musicales and soirees. While she had detractors—of which Lady Albertine was apparently one—it was obvious by the crush of this event that she commanded respect. Even his mother tried to attend her events.

"I requested a second dance."

"Y-you made me no promise, my lord,"

He gazed down at the beauty in his arms and noticed a faint cascade of freckles across her nose. *She is a curious mixture of confidence and shyness.* "What if I enjoyed the first dance?"

She gazed up at him, her eyes locking with his, but remained silent.

When the dance ended, he returned her to her sister and her friends.

"Thank you for the dance, Lord Wrotham," she said.

He bowed and kissed her hand. "The dance was my pleasure."

As he left, Lord Harrison nodded as he passed him, obviously hurrying to dance with Lady Priscilla. An uncomfortable twinge of possessiveness shot through Alex.

Looking around, he spotted Montgomery dancing with Lady Albertine's daughter. If he wasn't mistaken, he had danced with both. As far as Alex was concerned, that was more than enough to hold up their bargain with his mother; he had no interest in dancing any more this evening.

Catching his friend's attention, he nodded in the direction of the game room, signaling him he'd meet him there.

Chapter Four

"Daughter, there you are! Are you enjoying yourself?" Priscilla's father asked, handing her a lemonade and taking the seat next to her. "I observed you dancing with several eligible young men—including Lord Harrison and having not one, but two, dances with Lord Wrotham. I didn't notice him dancing with anyone else. Now I discover you hiding here with the wallflowers. Enlighten me."

"My feet have rebelled, Papa, and I sought refuge. These shoes are new, and they've worn a blister on my heel." She leaned down to rub the back of her left foot.

Her father gave a hearty laugh. "I confess, that was not what I expected to hear."

Priscilla gave a shy smile. She and her father had always enjoyed an amicable relationship. "Besides, most of these women are my friends. We've spent many a dance together holding up one wall or another," she replied before taking a sip of her lemonade.

"You are lovely, Priscilla, and I am pleased to see you finally discovering your assets." He reached over and hugged her.

"Thank you, Papa. I don't know exactly what to say."

"I can think of several things," he continued. "Like, what happened to the orange dress?"

Priscilla regarded her father's amused expression. "I lost the grip on my chocolate and spilled it. I was unable to move quickly enough, and despite our best efforts, there wasn't enough time to have the orange dress cleaned."

"Ah. I see. And the green dress? I have never noticed it before, and the way it lights up your face, it would not be one I would forget."

She stayed silent for a moment, unsure of what to say.

"Priscilla, I meant what I said to your mother earlier. The color is perfect for you. You look so much like my mother did when she was a young woman. I remember thinking her very beautiful when I was a child."

"I… uh… a-asked Madame Soyeuse to make it for me." She looked down and studied her fingernails. Admitting this to Papa seemed much harder than answering her mother, and she felt like he could see through the *accident*.

"Daughter, I do not mean to make you nervous or embarrassed." He reached over and squeezed her hand. "I understand. And that's all we should say about that. The other reason I stopped here was to see if you might be interested in playing whist with me."

"Papa, I would love to, but will Mama be all right with it?" Her father had always understood her, whereas her mother always seemed to want to make her into someone else—*herself*.

"Did you happen to notice your grandmama has arrived?"

"Yes," Priscilla said slowly. "But—"

"She will keep your mother occupied. Besides, your mother is thrilled with your success this evening and made sure I noticed you had danced twice with Lord Wrotham. And she noted that several other eligible young men had requested the pleasure of your company. As she would say, *Our wishes for our daughter Priscilla are on their way to being fulfilled.*" Amusement glinted in his eyes. "Is there something I should know… where Wrotham is concerned?"

"No, Papa. At least, I don't think so. He was just being nice," she assured him, although the earl's attention had confused her as well. Especially when he had brushed his hand lightly across her bare back, sending a fluttering sensation to the pit of her stomach. The sensation had nearly tongue-tied her!

Her mood lifted with her father's invitation to play whist with him. Dancing had been fun, but it had also been daunting and left her feeling perplexed. But cards were different from dancing. With cards, she was confident and in control. The night had unexpectedly taken a turn, and now it held promise. Even though betting at her parents' parties was frowned upon, playing cards provided an opportunity to practice her skill.

Her father gave an exaggerated sigh. "I expect we will be inundated with young men requesting your attention, sweet daughter." He stood and held out his arm. "Shall we visit the game room?"

They passed her mother, who dipped her head in acknowledgment while speaking to Grandmama. And Jane was dancing the reel with a new partner. Priscilla had her father to herself—a rare treat.

When they entered the room, Priscilla immediately noticed Lord Wrotham and Lord Montgomery at the billiard table, seemingly engrossed in a conversation between shots. She took a seat beside her father at an empty table. Two more players quickly joined them. While she studied the hand she had been dealt, she glanced across the room from beneath her lashes.

We danced twice, and he gave no indication he recognized Mr. Paul Smith from the Lyon's Den, she thought, confident that her alter ego had not been discovered. She planned to visit the den tomorrow. So far, the arrangement she had struck with the widow had worked fine. She took a hackney to the gambling den, exited at the door, and was ushered in. She surmised the widow had informed her floor staff to keep an eye on her. When her playing ended, Titan led her out the side to a hackney he had waiting for her.

"Priscilla, would you deal for us?" her father asked, handing her the deck.

Jolted back to the game, she accepted the deck. "I'm happy to, Papa," she said. Deftly, she cut the deck and smiled up at her father without glancing down at the cards dancing between her fingers, mindless minions of her brain. Confident they were shuffled, she dealt them.

Ten minutes later, her father laid down the king of diamonds, trumping the play before them. "I believe that's game for this round," he said before leaning closer to Priscilla. "I've noticed Wrotham glancing your way from across the room. It's as if he knows you. Are you certain tonight is the first time you've ever met him?"

Her father had taught her, so it was as easy to anticipate his moves as it probably was for him to know hers. She'd made sure he won a comfortable number of hands, to keep the attention off her. Now, it seemed the handsome Lord Wrotham and his constant staring at her from across the room had placed it on her. *Why would my father ask me that?*

"Yes, Papa. Of course, I've met his mother, Lady Wrotham, and her daughter, Lady Louisa, at Mama's events—but never Lord Wrotham." *Although I will never forget him.* "I recall the late earl attended one of Mama's musicales," she added. Priscilla always referred to the hated events as her *mother's* musicales because they were not something either she or her sister would ever choose to attend.

"I recall when the elder Wrotham attended. When the man died, young Wrotham was forced to return home from Paris, where he had been since the war ended. He was a close aide to Wellington," her father said. "An integral part of his staff, if I have that right."

"Losing a parent must be a hard thing to face when you return home," she murmured, reaching for her father's hand and giving it a gentle squeeze. Perusing her cards, she gently tucked a rogue curl behind her ear. Glancing up, she noticed Papa smiling at her.

"I believe it's your turn, daughter."

THE LAST THING Alex had expected to see was Lady Priscilla and her father sharing a card game in the game room. Women rarely ventured into the room, let alone on the arm of their fathers. Judging by their whispered conversation, it seemed father and daughter were extremely close, which intrigued him a little. According to gossip, the young woman couldn't sing a note, but it appeared she was talented with cards.

He looked once more and saw her shuffling the cards while her father looked on with pride. Lady Priscilla shuffled those cards with the efficiency of a well-trained player. It was clear her father had taught her. She couldn't sing like her mother, but she had a skill her father had taught her.

It was nice to see a father and daughter enjoying each other's company. Not many of Alex's friends' sisters had this type of relationship with their fathers.

"You are staring," Montgomery whispered loudly as he leaned over the table in Alex's direction and took aim with his cue stick. He watched in satisfaction as the two balls softly collided. "Although, I'll admit, she is a stunning young woman."

"Sorry. Her appearance in the game room with her father took me by surprise," Alex said, sizing up his next shot. "Just seems unusual."

Montgomery grunted. "Most unusual, I agree. But they seem very comfortable playing together. Perhaps he taught her."

"Hmm. You are right." Alex closed his eyes, forcing himself to clear his mind. He needed to stop thinking about Lady Priscilla. "Not to change the subject, but are you up for a visit to Cleveland Row tomorrow morning? I'd like to speak with the Black Widow, but I'm not anxious to go without a witness to the conversation," he said, taking his turn. "I've heard stories of people meeting with the widow and finding out they agreed to matrimony." He let out a nervous laugh.

"And, of course, you aren't interested in becoming leg-shackled." His friend chuckled. "I'll be happy to go with you, but if it's her cross hairs you're trying to avoid, I'd wager you're already in them."

Alex ran a hand through his hair in frustration. "I suppose you are right. But I want to make her aware of what happened yesterday. I got word from the magistrate this morning that he had the two men held in a cell, but they aren't talking. They tried to kill two peers of the realm and, at a minimum, will be rehomed at Newgate. The widow needs to know about Anders."

"They knew you had won big. Do you think someone tipped them off from inside the den?"

"I do. Anders. The man's a cheat. Worse, he planned to have us held up—possibly killed—just to regain his losses."

"Something doesn't add up. One of the men in the holdup said a 'she' paid them." Montgomery laid down his cue stick and picked up his cigar from a narrow table along the wall, where it had been resting while he played. He rolled it between his fingers before taking a slow puff.

"We don't have all of the answers, but the widow will want to know what type of crime is being perpetrated from her establishment."

"Mrs. Dove-Lyon has a reputation for separating fact from fiction. I almost feel sorry for Anders. When she finds out, I don't think he'll be able to count on her charity."

"Those men were out for blood. They could've killed Strafford.

Dr. Spencer managed to dig the bullet fragments from his side. He hopes he got them all, but Strafford has developed a fever. Doc said it could be touch and go." Alex sipped his brandy. "I believe Anders holds the answers to who was behind the attack."

Laughter at the card table drew his attention once again, and he watched Lady Priscilla tuck a strand of hair behind her ear. But it was the attractive, heart-shaped mole that caused his heart to skip a beat. It was unique. For a moment, he thought he remembered seeing a similar one.

What a ridiculous notion. He had never seen anything as unique as that on a face. Still, he needed to quell… what could he call this? His curiosity?

"Montgomery, did you get a good look at that young gambler, Mr. Smith, the other day?"

"Frankly, my attention was fixed on the card playing. But I think I got a good look."

"Did you notice anything odd about the sideburns?"

His friend sniggered. "Other than the thickness?"

"Well, there was that, but did you see anything else… maybe a mole?" he heard himself ask. What was wrong with him? He was pressing… but for what?

Montgomery hit his ball, laid down his cue stick, and picked up his drink. "A facial mole?"

"Yes." Alex felt his impatience rise.

"I'm trying to envision it, but I can't. I'm sorry. Why do you ask?"

"Never mind." He felt like an idiot. "Mayhap discussing Strafford has caused my imagination to work overtime. I was just wondering where he came from and thought something might trigger some level of recognition. Probably a new cit to the area." He took a lingering look in Priscilla's direction before turning back to the billiard game. He tapped his ball and missed. "You've beaten me again, old friend!"

"Billiards is a game of concentration. But judging from your plays,

I'd say your concentration has been somewhat cock-eyed. No one seems to be waiting for the billiard table. So, let's refill our cups and play again," Montgomery said before he polished off his drink. He was silent for a moment. "I don't think the opponents at the Burleson card table plan to stop playing anytime soon."

"Am I that obvious?" Alex sighed. "I'll do better in this next game. I hadn't expected her to show up in here."

"I've never seen you so taken with a female before," teased Montgomery.

"Simple infatuation, I'm afraid. That red hair and those eyes made it impossible to ignore her. But there's something else about her, and I cannot get a measure of what that is." Alex arranged the balls for the next game. "You have the most points, so you can start."

He watched Montgomery knock one cue ball into another, and it ricocheted into the red ball.

"Brilliant! Now if they stop where I want them to…" When it stopped, Alex aimed for the red ball, tapping it into a cue ball. "There! I'm determined to win this one. We're tied at two points each!"

"You can try!" Montgomery laughed heartily and gave Alex a friendly slap on the back. "What time do you want to visit the widow, tomorrow? Damn! You just cupped it. It's hard to believe it, but you are back in the game!"

Alex glanced up at his friend, grinning broadly. "I am!"

Chapter Five

The next afternoon

"Have you ever met the Black Widow?" Montgomery asked as he and Alex climbed into the coach.

"I cannot say that I have. Except for glimpses of her in the den. She shrouds her face with a black veil and dresses in black from head to toe."

The woman had a reputation for being clever and formidable. After all the warnings Montgomery had made, Alex had begun to believe they should have used a less obvious coach, but sat back and relaxed, as the coach had already begun lumbering down the drive. The black Wrotham coach had a gold W centered in a circle of small gold leaves and had become easy to recognize in town. Plush black leather covered the seats and dark purple velvet lined the walls. His father had had special springs installed to ensure a smooth ride over long distances, and it had become his mother's favorite coach.

"I wonder if Anders will be on the property when we get there," Alex murmured. "The man is a compulsive gambler. He thinks every game will be the one that delivers until it doesn't. He targeted us, thinking he would recoup his losses. But something doesn't add up. I keep coming back to the reference one of the ruffians made to a 'she.' Perhaps the widow will know something."

"I wonder if Anders has a mistress," Montgomery offered.

The coach stopped in front of the familiar blue building on Cleveland Row. Alex's footman, Williams, opened the door. "My lord, Strafford told me where to park."

"Pick us up in thirty minutes," Alex said.

"Yes, my lord."

As the coach pulled away, the door opened and Egeus, the frontman, welcomed them. "There's not too many in the gambling room, my lord."

"We're here to see Mrs. Dove-Lyon," Alex said.

"Is she expecting you?" the door manager asked.

"She replied to a message I sent, saying she looks forward to meeting," Alex said, his tone disclosing his irritation.

The man stiffened. "Follow me, my lord," Egeus said, closing the door behind them.

As they passed a large, windowed area, Alex peered down into the familiarity of the gaming scene below. He didn't smoke but found himself fascinated at the large cloud of cigar smoke lingering feet above the heads of the gambling patrons and staff. Certainly, he smelled the smoke when he was playing, but had not noticed its intensity. He must reek of it when he left there, he thought guiltily. Mason, his valet, visibly turned his nose up when he returned home from the den, but never said a word.

"It's so quiet up here," Montgomery whispered.

"It is. I wonder what accounts for that. It would be nice to have whatever works so well here, in our homes for dinner parties."

"Is it the glass that muffles the noise below?" Montgomery inquired.

Goodness. Montgomery seems more anxious than I do, Alex thought.

Does he know something I do not? Perhaps I should have listened more closely to his concerns.

Egeus regarded them before answering. "Aye, it keeps it quiet up here."

Indeed, it *was* quiet. Too quiet.

In minutes, they stood before a nondescript brown door leading to Mrs. Dove-Lyon's office area. Egeus opened it. "Lord Alex Wrotham and Viscount Sebastian Montgomery," he said before stepping back and closing the door behind him.

"My lords. I'm glad to finally have a chance to meet you both." Had they not discussed the widow's dark appearance, it might have startled them.

"You as well, Mrs. Dove-Lyon. We appreciate your taking the time to meet with us," Montgomery said.

"May I ask why we are meeting?" the woman inquired.

"Yes, most certainly. We feel we have some important information, and it has to do with one of your… frequent customers," Alex said. You would think he was meeting with the Queen of England, with this much formality.

"I find myself most interested in what you have to offer," the widow said, gesturing for them to sit.

The men sat in matching velvet armchairs in front of the desk. Alex laid his cane next to his chair. A red velvet-covered settee with carved golden arms sat to his left. It perfectly matched the red theme that ran throughout the gambling den. Rich, dark red carpet with matching velvet curtains covered the floor and windows. A pale red wallpaper with a cherub pattern covered the wall. To the right of the settee sat a gilt-laden cart set with a silver tea service.

"May I offer either of you tea, or perhaps something stronger?" She casually directed their attention to the liquor cabinet sitting against the wall behind them, to the left of the door. It was a large, ornate cabinet with rose-colored glass panes set in dark mahogany.

"Yes, perhaps a brandy would suit," Montgomery answered before

Alex could decline. "Thank you, Mrs. Dove-Lyon."

"And you, Lord Wrotham. Brandy for you as well?"

Alex nodded.

She reached up and pulled a dark brown cord. A moment later, Egeus reentered the room, and the widow indicated the liquor cabinet. The man nodded and poured each of the three a liberal glass of brandy, taking the widow her glass before serving the men. He left as quickly as he had appeared, and Alex assumed he was waiting in the hall. There would be no chance to get lost in the hall when they left. A pity. He would have liked to have seen more of this floor. It was where she oversaw her operations from.

"You were saying?" she asked after taking a sip. Pointedly, she looked at Alex.

"Two nights ago, we were set upon by two highwaymen shortly after leaving here. I would not have connected them, except I recalled seeing one of the men talking with Lord Anders at the door, shortly before our game. And I had also seen that same man escorting his wife in town, as she shopped. The second man was not familiar to me. They attempted to rob me when we left here—and knew I had a good deal of money on my person." Weirdly, Alex was glad to finally have that off his chest and hoped she would feel as concerned as he was. It had bothered him much more than he had realized.

"I hate to hear such a thing about Lord Anders. He has been a patron for many years," she said in measured words. "But you thwarted the robbery, I assume."

"We did," Montgomery said.

"And you feel certain Anders is behind it."

"My gut tells me so," Alex replied. "I have learned over the years to follow my instincts."

"We feel especially so having noticed him meeting with the man Lord Wortham mentioned that very evening and feel certain he arranged to have his losses returned to him when we left, even if it meant killing us," Montgomery added.

"I see."

Alex would swear he saw her face redden with anger behind the black veil.

"Was anyone injured?" she asked.

"Yes. My driver was nearly killed before we could help him. The stop was planned. We were attacked on the darkest part of the journey into town. I've seen the other man but cannot place him… yet." He paused and took a sip of his brandy to let what he had said settle. "I feel sure a savvy businesswoman such as yourself would want to know about this type of thing."

"Most assuredly. I do not tolerate such… mischief and will see that it's dealt with immediately." She paused. "I am assuming these men are still in custody. To be fair, I will speak with them and gain my impression."

Alex started to say something but held his tongue and nodded. If the widow wanted to speak with someone jailed, he imagined she had the power and connections to do just that. Her presence could intimidate some, especially those familiar with the staff she employed. "They are with the magistrate—who probably has them jailed. I plan to pursue charges and will see Anders rehomed… either in Newgate or in the colonies."

She nodded slightly. "Yes. I'm quite certain that is within your power." Smiling, she pointed to the drink. "You drink but have no thirst for it. That is good for you, bad for my business."

Alex chuckled. "Yes, I understand. But I prefer to keep my wits about me when I gamble."

"I've noticed you haven't lost."

Alex was surprised by her comment. Montgomery was right. She had him in her sights. He wondered if she would share any information and ventured cautiously. "I noticed a new player. I believe his name is Paul Smith. He played two days ago, didn't he?"

She examined her manicured hands and remained quiet for a moment. "I believe you are right. I can check for sure, but I believe he might have been here two days ago."

"He is new to your establishment."

"He... is."

Alex leaned forward. "I'm rather curious about the young man. He has tremendous talent. Can you tell me where is he from? Perhaps I know his family."

She gave a hollow laugh and leaned back in her chair. "Lord Wortham, as you can imagine, I cannot give the names of my clientele to... anyone. It would be most unseemly." She briefly examined her nails again, obviously contemplating the rest of her response. "As a member of the peerage, you will know many that you see in here." She regarded him with a thin smile. "But if there are those you do not know but wish to know... that is totally within your control."

Her smile irked him, but he kept his tone light. "I know when I've hit a dead end," he said, placing the brandy on the table between him and Montgomery. "Mr. Smith was a curiosity. My concern is Anders. He is trouble. I didn't call him out, but he cheated while we played."

"How?"

"Your dealer saw it. The man palmed more than one card—twice. The second time, the dealer commented that he had accidentally taken an additional card, and the man went overboard with excuses. Despite his efforts, he lost. Then attempted to ambush us returning home, determined to regain his losses."

"How positively awful. I assure you, Lord Wrotham, I plan to deal with Lord Anders."

He wanted to feel sorry for Anders, but it wasn't in him. "I'm sure you knew about the cheating. But the man is dangerous. Be careful." He felt her watching him.

"There is one thing I can share with you—and it may be more important than you realize," she said.

Montgomery leaned forward. "A name?"

"I wish I knew the name. I have my suspicions, and I am certain she exists. Anders has a mistress. Rumor is she is more than a mistress—but I don't know anything for certain. But you have the resources to find out more."

Alex would have sworn he saw her smile beneath the black veil.

"They mentioned *she* in the attack. That has been the one thing that made no sense," Montgomery interjected.

"Until things are resolved for him, remember that Anders is desperate, and desperate people do stupid things. Although what he did will cost him. And that he used my establishment will cost him." She drew a slow breath. "Watch your backs, my lords. That is all I know." She stood and left the room.

The meeting was over. It had been an exchange of information. The door opened and Egeus entered. "Follow me," he said.

As they walked past the window, Montgomery glanced down and then tapped his friend's arm. "Wrotham, look. Isn't that Mr. Smith? It appears he's cashing out," he whispered.

Alex noticed Titan, the floorman, waiting for Smith at the front door, where a hackney sat waiting. He wondered if they were making sure the young man met no ill fate on his way home. "How did we miss him?" Alex muttered. Then, more loudly, "Egeus, is there an entrance into the gambling den downstairs?"

Seeming to sense their hurry, the man continued down the stairs and replied, "No. I must escort you from the building, my lord. However, you may enter the gambling den by the front door."

How odd to restrict visitors in such a manner, Alex thought.

"There he goes," Montgomery said, pointing to Mr. Smith in the window of the hackney that had just left.

Determined, Alex whistled for his coach. The driver immediately pulled up to the curb. "Williams, follow that hackney," he said as they got inside. Once seated, Alex tapped on the ceiling and the coach lurched forward.

Chapter Six

Once her hand ended, Priscilla opened the small note Titan had handed her earlier.

Yer ride is here.

She glanced up at the clock. Three hours was long enough. "Gentlemen, I'm afraid I must leave." Her announcement was met with groans and demands to give them a chance to win their losses back.

"Mr. Wilson," she rasped in her male voice, "we have played several times, and I find I cannot afford to lose more to you."

The older man smiled at her comment. "Yes, yes. Understandable. But I would like a rematch, Mr. Smith."

Priscilla infrequently lost on purpose—when the cost was minimal to her winnings—to seed hope with her opponents. Consistent with her goal, she retained most of her take. "Absolutely, kind sir. I look forward to playing you again if you are in the house." With that, she stood and collected her chips.

As Titan led her to the door, he whispered, "Mrs. Dove-Lyon had a party ask about you, so she felt an earlier exit might be in your best interest."

"Who?" she asked, instantly aware her voice had been higher.

"The widow didn't say," the floorman replied. "The driver knows where to take you."

Mrs. Dove-Lyon had ordered the carriage earlier on several occasions to protect Priscilla's safety. Realizing this, she refrained from asking more. "Thank you, Titan," she intoned in her male voice.

Once inside the carriage, she took a deep breath, relaxed, and silently congratulated herself on her winnings. Just shy of two hundred pounds! She could scarcely believe it. Usually, her winnings were less than that—except for a few days ago when she had bested Lord Markham. The rogue had even tried to cheat!

Boys' sharp taunts and a dog's bark pierced her thoughts, making her push back the curtains to peek. A young girl, who could not be more than seven years old, and her raggedy black dog were fending off a group of older boys. The little girl was sobbing and trying to block the rocks and sticks being thrown by the boys. The dog's snout and ears were bloodied, probably from defending itself and the girl.

Almost standing in the carriage, Priscilla rapped on the ceiling, determined to get out as quickly as she could. "Stop," Priscilla yelled, almost forgetting to use her male voice. The old man driving the hack obeyed and slowed down. Before the carriage stopped, Priscilla flung open the door, leaped out, and crossed the street. Walking up to the boys, she stood almost nose to nose with the eldest boy and placed her hands on her hips. "I said to stop. Stop at once," she demanded, doing her best to maintain her cover.

"Look, guvnor, this ain't none of yer concern," the biggest boy said before picking up a stick and slinging it at the girl. Then he crossed cross his arms in a belligerent stance. His soot-covered pants barely covered his legs, and his coat hung tattered on his back. His stringy ginger hair fell in his eyes, and his broken, bloodied lip supported his willingness to fight.

"I said to… stop!" she rasped loudly, causing the three boys to step back. The smallest one dropped his weaponry and fled. Fury had overtaken her, only fed when she glanced at the driver and noticed he sat watching. *But then, he thought his passenger was a man, so he would not have offered help,* she reminded herself.

"They 'urt m'dog... sir," the little girl managed in between hiccupping sobs. "Red is trying to 'urt us." Tears streamed a path down her dirty face.

"Does your dog have a name?" Priscilla asked, swallowing past the lump in her throat. She surmised the boy's name was Red, probably because of his hair.

"This 'ere dog ain't hers. She found 'er," the older boy said. "So, oi can do what oi want to do with it."

"I don't agree with you... Red," Priscilla replied, anger lacing her voice. "I asked you to leave off!"

The boy's face reddened.

"I call 'er P...Penelope. P...Penny fer short," the girl stammered, ignoring him.

The black dog had stubby legs and a large girth. But Priscilla noticed that she moved surprisingly fast, snarling at the boys and doing her best to protect the little girl, even if it meant being hit by rocks.

"What is your name, child, and where do you live?" Priscilla had squatted down so she could see into the little girl's eyes. She fought the impulse to hold her close and comfort her. The girl's eyes were hazel, and her face held a light dusting of freckles. Her light brown hair had soft curls that fell at her back, but most of it looked matted, and her lavender dress was torn. Spots of blood soaked the bottom of her sleeves where she had been protecting her dog.

"M'name's Maggie, sir," she finally answered.

"That's a very pretty name. Where do you live, Maggie? I can take you and your dog home."

"She ain't got no 'ome," a dark-haired boy spoke up from behind Red. "'Er mum died, and she and the dog live where they find a spot."

Priscilla nodded, understanding, and fighting past the knot that formed in her throat. "Is that what happened, Maggie?"

The girl nodded, and more tears flowed. "My mum died, and Penny is all I have. She gave me a couple of dings... I hid dem so the man wouldn't dake dem."

"The man?" Priscilla asked, unsure of to whom the child referred.

"A big man pulled me away from my mum and took me to that building. He wouldn't let me go home."

The small child pointed to a brick factory that stood above most of the buildings, a couple of streets over. The Chantry Sewing Factory. Her father had mentioned it when he spoke of child labor, she thought, remembering how she had believed the owner heartless.

"He locked you in there?" Priscilla fought to maintain her charade.

"It was dark, and everyone was gone. I cried for Mummy, and Penny found me. She showed me how to crawl out a hole in da wall." The child trembled at the recollection.

Priscilla was horrified. To take a child and lock them in a building, intent on keeping them there as labor, was despicable. Her father would never approve of such a thing. He often voiced objections to child labor.

She took out her handkerchief and looked Maggie in the eyes. "Then I shall take you and Penny with me. We shall see what we can do to fix Penny's wounds."

Without waiting another minute, she opened the door to the hack and helped Penny inside. Maggie followed.

"Mr. Smith, oi will 'ave to charge ye extra to transport..." the driver protested.

Priscilla reached into her pocket and withdrew a shilling, tossing it to him as she had seen her father do. "I understand," she said. She started to close the door and changed her mind. Turning around, she fished several shillings from her pocket. "It goes against my better nature to give you boys anything, considering how unkind you are.

But maybe you will think about how to help people rather than how to cause them pain." She handed each of them a shilling and gave an extra one to the dark-headed one. "Give this one to the little boy that ran."

The boy accepted the shillings in his hand and stared up at her, his mouth agape.

"Yer giving us a twelver? Oi ain't ne'er 'ad this much money to keep." The boy looked at the shillings in his hand and back at her.

"Do you have a name?"

"Oi do. 'Tis Jake."

"Jake, I know this isn't much, but maybe you and your brother can use it. And find something nicer to do for fun."

"Oi will, mister. And oi'll remember what ye said," Jake said, clutching both coins tightly.

"Stow it, Jake," Red sniped.

"You stow it! The quality was being nice," Jake snapped back. He looked up at Priscilla. "Would ye tell Maggie we're sorry?"

"I will," she said, watching the boys run to join the other one before climbing into the carriage.

The hack lurched and moved forward at a faster clip. For a few minutes, no one said a word.

"I will take you to the kitchen to find some food, but first, I need to ask you to wait in the barn with Penny, until I let the cook know about you. Will you stay there, Maggie?"

She sat there clutching Penny, who had licked the tears from her face.

"Yes, sir."

"Cook and my cousin, Lady Priscilla, will be caring for you. They will make sure you both get a good meal, a bath, and decent clothing."

The little girl wiped her face and turned to her dog. "Hear dat, Penny? Mummy said someone would help us."

I need to figure out how I'm going to explain their presence and keep her from going to an orphanage. Maggie can't stay in the barn. A cold thought ran the length of Priscilla's spine. Maggie had seen her disguise—because Mr. Smith had rescued her.

She turned to the child. "Maggie, can you keep a secret?" Oh God! She hated herself for asking a child to lie, but the situation demanded it. "Can you do that?"

The child nodded.

"It's unfair to have to ask this, but do you know what a secret is?" Priscilla pressed.

"Mum said it was something you can't tell," the child said softly. "I ne'er told Mum's secrets."

"Your mum… had secrets? Wh…what did she die of?"

"She got very sick. Mummy coughed lots of blood."

Consumption, Priscilla thought. The child might need to be quarantined. Cook and Mary would help her, and they would know what to do for Maggie. She didn't appear to have picked up her mother's illness. "How long ago did your mum die?" Priscilla asked.

"It's been a while." Maggie held up four fingers. "This many weeks."

Priscilla relaxed. The child showed no signs of illness. In fact, under the dirt, she looked healthy. But leaning back in the seat, Priscilla began to rethink her purpose with the winnings. She had given the three boys money, even though they had hurt both Maggie and Penny. She would wager they were also homeless. And from the level of soot on Red's clothing, she imagined his life to be much harder than anyone she knew. With her pin money and her winnings, she was accumulating quite a bit of cash. Perhaps there was something that she could do to help children and, at the same time, gain the independence she craved. An orphanage entered her mind—but not just any orphanage. It had to be one that could help the children gain decent livings—not working in chimneys or factories. And certainly not locked in one! She would speak to her father—as soon as she could conjure a suitable story. For now, she would stay on course.

Priscilla failed to notice the black lacquered coach that followed them. It remained a few carriages behind.

"WHAT DO YOU make of that?" Alex said as they watched the hackney pull to the corner and drop off Mr. Smith, the girl, and the dog. As the trio approached the homes, he watched Mr. Smith lead them down the drive of the Millers' house next to the Burlesons' townhouse, making their way to the mews. The Millers had gone to their country estate for the holiday season, leaving their home vacant. It was a perfect way for Lady Priscilla to slip in and out of her real home—and her identity as Mr. Smith if they were one and the same. He couldn't swear to it—yet. But he was almost certain after seeing her play cards with her father and noting the vast similarities, as well as the absurd amount of facial hair—Mr. Smith had to be Lady Priscilla.

"I saw it, but I cannot believe it. Even more, he gave money to the boys," Montgomery observed. "The dog looked pretty beaten up."

She has a kind heart, Alex thought. "Yes, *that,* but what else did you notice?"

Montgomery looked at him and smiled. "I think Lady Priscilla has some explaining to do. And it may start with how she found the girl and the dog."

Having constantly rebuked himself for his wild suspicions, Alex now knew they hadn't been unfounded. Only now he was burdened with deciding *what to do* with his knowledge. And what about his fascination with Lady Priscilla? But fascination was all he felt, he told himself. Even so, there was no way could he allow her to go to Cleveland Row—escorted or not. He imagined her father would be just as shocked. Why was she doing it? He would need that from her. But first, he wanted to gain her trust, or he risked driving her away.

"You haven't spoken to the Bow Street Runners lately," Montgomery said. "I'd suggest we cover that base. Perhaps they can find out some information about Anders's mistress. I, for one, need to know more."

"I agree." Alex tapped on the roof of his carriage and leaned out the window. "Williams, please take us to the Bow Street Runners."

"Yes, my lord," his driver said, turning away from the street in Mayfair and heading into town.

They arrived at the office housing the Runners and saw the person they wished to speak with walk into the building. Alex tapped on the ceiling, and the carriage pulled to the curb and stopped. "We'll be out shortly Williams," Alex said, as the two men walked into the building.

"How many I help you?" the man at the front desk asked.

"I'm Lord Wrotham. This is Lord Montgomery. He and I need to speak to Michael Bennett if he is here."

"Let me check. He mentioned having a meeting outside the city," the man said.

"When we leave here, I'll catch a hack to the Home Office. I'd like to speak to Kitterman," Montgomery said. "I can take care of this. You told your mum you'd escort her and your sister to town."

"Let Williams drop me off at home and take you where you'd like to go," Alex offered.

"No. Your mother enjoys her carriage, and it's not hard to figure out why," Montgomery said with a laugh. "I wouldn't want to be the one displacing her."

"You're right. I had forgotten about the promise to escort them to town."

"Lord Wrotham, Lord Montgomery, thank you for stopping by. I was going to be locating you," Bennett said, entering the room.

"We came up with some more information today and thought it

could help. It could be related or not... but I want to know more," Alex said.

"And what would that information be?" Bennett asked.

"Lord Anders hired two highwaymen to ambush us on the way home to retrieve his losses, and my driver was nearly killed."

"I assume the two men the magistrate asked us to hold are the two you are speaking of," Bennett replied.

"Yes. And you will probably also get a visit from the Black Widow, Mrs. Dove-Lyon, since Anders most likely transacted this at her club," Montgomery interjected. "But we digress."

"It was the Black Widow who mentioned Anders has a mistress but offered no details," Alex continued. "However, the fact that she mentioned it gave me the impression this woman could be more important than just his mistress."

"This could help," Bennett replied. "Up to now, Mrs. Marble has led us on a merry chase and has not been seen with anyone but theater staff, which is unusual, considering her reputation. I have not seen Anders with her. One of the two men the magistrate confined in the hold could help, because I recognize the tall, hatchet-faced one. I saw them speaking with Anders four days past. When were you set upon by these men?"

"Three days ago," Montgomery replied. "Do you think there could be a connection?"

"Find out everything you can—and please let one of us know as soon as you find out anything," Alex interjected. "The taller man mentioned that *she* told them they could have what they found. We cannot be certain who *she* is, but what you suggest makes sense. Perhaps she and Anders's mistress are the same person."

"Whew! That would be quite a connection," Bennett said.

"But we need proof," Montgomery stressed. "Irrefutable proof."

"Do you have anything else?" Alex asked.

"We are working on it. In other words, no," Bennett said.

"It feels like we need the information even sooner. Can you put more men on this?" Alex asked.

"We will do our best. I promise." Bennett pulled out his pocket watch and checked the time. "I apologize for being rude, gentlemen. But I must meet someone, and it's important."

"Understandable. We both have places to go as well," Alex said, tipping his hat.

As they walked back to the coach, Montgomery stopped. "I have to say something, Wrotham."

"Is something the matter?" Alex had sensed Montgomery was bothered about something, but the best way to get him to talk was to wait him out.

"Yes... well, maybe," Montgomery admitted. "I'm troubled by the Black Widow's comments about your gaming—specifically, your winning. Add to that her observations about your aversion to drinking, and it seems she's tagged you for something. Just be careful."

"Her comments piqued my interest as well, and your warnings flooded my head. I'll be very careful. With my father's debts mostly paid off, I was thinking to limit my playing—unless an unusual situation arises. I cannot think what that would be. I would like to go back a time or two. I don't want her to think she ran us off."

Montgomery gave a small, derisive laugh. "Honestly, who would care? Better than becoming leg-shackled to a woman you can't abide—right?"

"Sound point, my friend." Distracted, Alex twirled the top of his cane in his hand. "What do you say we meet tomorrow at Gentleman Jackson's for a little sport? I need the exercise and some time away from the house."

A smile stretched across Montgomery's face. "That's a great idea. Exercise would be good for us both. I know you have promised to meet your mother and accompany her"—he glanced up with a blank look—"I cannot recall where, but I want to stop by the Home Office to see Kitterman. It's a couple of streets over, so I'll walk."

Alex chuckled. "I cannot either. It was something she roped me into doing. Let's meet at three o'clock tomorrow. We can have dinner at Dolly's Chop House afterward." *It'll give me time to sort this out,* he reasoned. *And it'll give me time away from my mother and her cloying need to be accompanied everywhere.*

"Sounds good. I'll see you tomorrow at Jackson's," Montgomery called out as they turned and headed in opposite directions.

Alex glanced back at his friend for a moment before turning around. Maybe Montgomery was right about the Lyon's Den. The widow's familiarity made him uncomfortable. And then there was the matter of Mr. Smith—*no, Lady Priscilla*. He couldn't deny an attraction to her… but that was all it was. He was sure of it. As a gentleman, he could not knowingly let her get into a bad situation, which was highly possible if she persisted with this foolishness at the Lyon's Den. As he thought about it, he realized he needed to tell her father. She would hate him for that, but it was the right thing to do. *Tomorrow.*

Chapter Seven

The next morning

"My lady, I have your biscuits and hot tea," Mary said, walking in and setting the tray on a small table next to Priscilla's chair, in front of the fireplace. "Your little Maggie is downstairs in the kitchen. I bathed her and altered one of your old dresses I found in the nursery. Cook fed both she and her dog, and they ate like they had not eaten in an age. The dog won't leave her side."

Mary stood in front of Priscilla… waiting. It was her way of returning a problem Priscilla had given her that the maid couldn't solve.

"I'm sorry, Mary. I've created a muddle this time. But I couldn't leave her to fend for herself. The bigger boys were throwing sticks and stones at the child and the dog."

"You've got a big heart, my lady. But now you've got a big problem, as well," the maid said matter-of-factly.

"You are right—and it's my difficulty. You and Cook have helped so much already." This was a big mess. When Priscilla brought Maggie and Penny home, she had made temporary provisions with Mary for the child to sleep in the servants' quarters in one of the empty rooms. But still, she hadn't discussed any of it with her mother or her father. That needed to happen today… but first, she needed to speak with Maggie. How much should she tell Maggie? Would the child give her secret away?

"You say she is in the kitchen with Cook?" Priscilla asked.

"Yes, my lady."

Priscilla's head pounded. She desired a hot cup of tea and a warm bed where she could snuggle beneath the covers. However, she had to set this to rights and get Maggie and her dog squared away. It was the right thing. Most orphaned children ended up in workhouses or worse. Priscilla couldn't allow that to happen to this child. But she needed a plausible story to share with her parents or her ruse was up—and she didn't know what would happen to Maggie and her dog.

Priscilla knew she should have already spoken to her father. That she had waited would only make him angrier, but she was sure he would help. Mother's reaction could be unpredictable, and that was a problem by itself—the thought of which made her head pound harder.

"I will speak with Papa, but give me time to get rid of this dreadful headache."

"I'll ask Cook to fix you a remedy."

"Yes. That would help. Thank you, Mary," she said, accepting a cup of tea and leaning back into the warmth of her chair. Priscilla enjoyed staring into a roaring fire—finding it mesmerizing, almost transporting. It provided refuge on days when Mama tested her forbearance, or when a social event had become too painful to stand. The licking flames sucked her in, mind and body. The newly stoked fire roared with color, warmth, and harmony. Priscilla tucked her feet beneath her morning robe and relaxed as she sipped her tea.

With eyes closed, she drank in the heat of the fire. Unbidden, the Earl of Wrotham's face floated in her mind, sending a jolt of warmth through her. Adding to her pleasure was the memory of his scent—

vanilla and patchouli—and, as if he were with her now, she hummed the waltz they had danced to. She could almost feel his arms tighten around her as they swirled to the music, igniting waves of fluttery feelings in the pit of her stomach.

How had this man invaded her mind and body? As pleasant as it was, she would never truly gain his notice, making her mind's constant manifestation of him torture. Not even her private dreams provided refuge from his company.

Last night's dream had had them waltzing onto her mother's piazza, where he had kissed her beneath the starry night sky. His warm lips met hers, causing her pulse to quicken and her body to quiver from his heat.

With a jerk, she opened her eyes and put her hand to her head.

Could her imaginary kisses even compete with his real kiss? There was no indication that would ever occur—but if it did, it would be a dream come true.

"My lady?" Mary prodded.

"I'm sorry, Mary," Priscilla said, setting down her cup. "I became so comfortable I fell asleep. But I need your help." She stood, straightening her robe. "Is Cook in the kitchen?"

"Yes. The child is with her."

"Oh dear. I will be back as soon as I can. If Mama stops in, tell her I'm indisposed." At the shocked look on Mary's face, Priscilla paused. "Mama never questions you. She will tell you to send me to see her."

"She *trusts* me, my lady."

Mary's voice held an edge, but Priscilla ignored it. The woman had been more of a friend than a servant. Lately, Mary had lied for her. "That was wrong. I apologize, Mary." She walked to her door and peered into the hall. "I'll take the servants' stairs and will be as quick as I can." Without waiting for a response, Priscilla stepped across the hall into the servants' stairwell, closing the door gently and heading down the steps.

"Priscilla," a familiar voice called out.

She froze and turned to see her sister in the stairwell. Relief washed over her. "Jane, what are you doing on these steps?"

"I could ask you the same thing, Cilla. Mother is looking for you. When I went to find you, I saw you slip across the hallway and duck into the servants' stairwell." Jane continued a few more steps and stopped. "Where did you find the girl and the dog?"

Priscilla froze, before slowly turning around. "What—"

"Come on, Cilla, you know I read you like a book. Besides, I was in the kitchen earlier, and I saw them both. Poor Cook is beside herself trying to hide the dog—who insists on being next to the girl and won't remain outside. When the door opens, she slips in with a maid or a footman—all of whom adore both the child and the dog, according to Cook."

"I... uh... I..."

"Cilla, I saw you slip into your room, dressed like a man—not bad, I might add," her sister said saucily. "At first, I thought it was a man and became concerned, but when I peeped in, I saw you pulling off the mustache."

Priscilla's eyes rounded. "When did you..."

"Does it matter? I've told no one. And I don't intend to... if you share what's going on with me."

Cold fear washed over Priscilla. "You wouldn't tell, Jane."

"No, not if you tell me. We've never kept secrets from each other—especially since we are both so persecuted by Mama's ambitions for us," Jane said gently. "Besides... I'd like to help. Where did you find *her*?"

Priscilla started to speak but closed her mouth, deciding it was better to hear what Jane had to say. If her sister had seen her, maybe others knew as well.

"Fine. I saw you climb out of a hack and walk from the corner. I had been taking some flowers to Mrs. Smythe, as a favor to Mama.

And this odd young man with a child and a dog climbed out of a hackney, and the three of them walked to our house… and slipped in the servants' door. I came in the front door, and when I reached the landing, I saw you dart into your room—dressed as a man. So, tell me. Who is she, and how can I help?"

Pricilla's eyes welled with tears. For as much as her sister was younger than she, they had always been there for each other. Jane hated Mama's exhibitions as much as Priscilla did. But standing in front of the *haute ton* and performing without real talent didn't traumatize Jane as it did Priscilla. If Jane had not been by her side, Priscilla would never have made it through those songs. She shuddered.

"Maggie. Her name is Maggie, and the dog is Penny. I found her and the dog protecting themselves from rocks and sticks being hurled at them by other children. Her mother died almost a month ago from consumption. I need to tell Papa, but I'm not sure *what* to tell him."

Jane crossed her arms. "Why are you dressing like a man?" she demanded.

"You do get to the meat of it, don't you, Jane?" Priscilla gave a soft shrug of her shoulder. "I plan to eventually have my own home and need money. You know my only talent is cards, so I've been playing at the Lyon's Den."

Jane took a swift intake of breath. "What? Surely you are making that up. Mama will lock you in your room until you are old and gray if she finds out. And what about the dangers? That's a gambling den!"

"Yes. It *is*," Priscilla said, her tone one of resignation. "It's all safe. I met with the widow… Mrs. Dove-Lyon. She agreed to allow me to come if I promised certain things. I must arrive in a hackney and let her men put me on a hackney to return. And I don't go during the evening. I leave before it gets dark. I also don't stay more than a couple of hours."

"That still sounds bad."

"I must tell Papa about Maggie and Penny. And I don't want to divulge my secret."

Jane stood there for a moment before looking up with a big smile. "You'll have to ask Maggie not to tell your secret, because she saw you as a man. But you can say we both found her on a shopping trip to town. I went with Mary while you were gone... but no one knows you weren't with us. And Mary is already helping you."

Priscilla knew Mary wouldn't appreciate being brought into one more lie, but in for a penny, in for a pound, as the saying went. "You would help me?"

"You are my sister. Of course, I would. But I want you to stop going to the Lyon's Den."

"Please don't ask that of me. It's easy money for me, and you know there have been no suitors. I'm going to be a spinster, and I might as well find something to do that has meaning."

"What do you mean?" Jane asked.

"Can we discuss this later, dear sister? I need your help. Follow me." Priscilla was anxious to get to the kitchen. "Mother could be down here at any minute, and I need to get to speak with Cook and Maggie and fix this."

"Introduce me to Maggie. I have an idea," Jane said.

"Care to share?"

"Trust me, sister. I will keep your secret. But promise me, you'll speak with Papa about what you are doing."

Jane didn't wait for an answer. They walked into the kitchen together.

"You must be Maggie." Jane kneeled to eye level with the little girl. "My sister wants to help you."

"Maggie, that's a sweet dog," Priscilla said gently. "She is quiet but won't go anywhere you don't. We don't want her to get into trouble, so let's take her outside for a few minutes."

"The nice lady named Mary said you gave me this pretty dress," the little girl said, drawing closer to her dog and biting thoughtfully on her forefinger.

"It looks nice on you. And I'll bet we can find a few more and have them adjusted for you. But I wanted to ask you a favor," Priscilla began.

Jane interrupted. "What my sister is saying is our cousin was in town briefly but didn't want anyone to know. However, when he saw you, he couldn't leave you there, so he brought you here and asked if we could help you. Would that be all right with you?"

"Are you going to let me live here?" Maggie asked.

"I must speak with my father. But I must ask that you not tell anyone you met my cousin. It's most important." Priscilla winced. She hated asking this small child to lie. "Can I count on you?"

The child's brow wrinkled, and she appeared to struggle. "I... I dink so. But Mummy told me to never lie."

"And we don't want you to lie," Jane interjected smoothly. "That would be most improper. If someone asks you if you met our cousin, you may tell them so. But if they ask anything else, tell them Lady Priscilla and Lady Jane have been helping you. Will that do?"

The child gave a smile of relief and nodded. "'Cause that is the druth. I promise."

Priscilla swallowed. She intended to speak with her father as soon as Maggie and the dog were settled. *More lies—this time to my father,* she thought. Whatever made her think engaging in this charade was a good idea? The only silver lining had been rescuing Maggie and Penny—an impulsive act that had made her realize she wanted to spend her money on children, like Maggie, not on herself. Somehow, just admitting that to herself made what she had ahead of her more palatable.

"Do you need me to go to Papa with you?" Jane asked, jarring her from her thoughts.

"Jane, I feel horrid dragging you into all of this. But yes, if you would, it might lend the credibility I need. I cannot let Maggie down."

"I love you, Cilla. You know that. And you know you would do it for me. Besides, Cook has found a temporary location for Maggie. The young servant Mama dismissed last month had a small room upstairs, and according to the housekeeper, it is still vacant."

"Oh goodness! Mrs. Smithers knows, too?"

"She does and adores Maggie. While she isn't fond of having a dog in the house, the other servants are willing to help."

"Thank you, Jane. I would much appreciate your being there when I speak with Papa," Priscilla said. *This will be my last lie,* she promised herself.

Chapter Eight

"My lord, you asked that I made sure you were awake with the sun," Mason said, drawing back the heavy green draperies. "Your bath will be ready in fifteen minutes."

Alex awoke and stared at the top of his dark, canopied bed. Once he opened his curtain, the chilly air would usher in the day ahead. He was determined to meet the encounter head-on. Irrationally, however, meeting with Lord Burleson and telling him his daughter was dressing like a man and sneaking into an illicit gaming den made him nervous—not a feeling he liked. Suddenly more seemed to ride on this meeting than he had initially considered, and he wasn't looking forward to it.

Would she see this as a betrayal? A chill traveled down his spine. They had spoken little, yet there had been a connection when they were at her parents' soiree. He was sure of it. What other reason could there be for her to be on his mind constantly? If he spoke to Lady Priscilla's father, he would need to be careful, gauging every word before he uttered it. Yet his stomach churned. He needed to decide his next move. If he told Lord Burleson, and it went badly, she would be lost.

He wavered on whether to court her—lured by constant thoughts of large lavender eyes fringed by long lashes, and beautiful red hair he imagined running his fingers through. Seeing her would come with a set of expectations, and Alex didn't need a wife in his life. He enjoyed his freedom and his involvement with the Crown. Of course, since becoming earl, he'd no longer accepted missions, but there was work behind the scenes—important work if England were to stay ahead of those stirring unrest in his country.

He also had family commitments. He had promised his father many years ago to take care of the earldom, and planned to take Thomas under his wing. As a second son, Alex felt sure his brother would have more entertaining activities on his mind—and he had chosen a career in law. But without another heir, Alex owed continuity to his mother, who had just come out of mourning. She was doing her best to make the most of her life and continually accepted invitations to social events, always expecting him to attend—exposing him to her devious matchmaking. Adding to that, Louisa was already being outfitted to debut into Society. If only he could get his mother to focus on that and stop the matchmaking. If only he could make *that* happen.

A wife was out of the picture.

"Thank you, Mason," he murmured, placing his feet on the hunter-green Aubusson rug and willing himself to stand.

"It's overcast and damp, my lord," the valet said, pouring water into the shaving basin. "My aching back tells me to expect snow. Perhaps I should summon the carriage for your meeting."

"Dash it! I had hoped for a sunnier day." Alex glanced out the window and winced. Reproachful news was always easier to take on a sunnier day. "Your back is usually correct in these matters, Mason. The carriage would be much appreciated. Make it the unmarked one. And ask Smithers to have a liveried footman ride along with Williams. Strafford is still recuperating, so Williams will drive."

"The unmarked one it is, your lordship," Mason said, applying the hot towel on Alex's face to soften the beard. "Your mother is in the dining room breaking her fast."

"Thank you for letting me know."

A short time later, Alex entered the dining room, immediately enjoying the aroma of eggs, rashers, puddings, fruits, and sweet bread lining the sidebar. "Good morning, Mother," he said, helping himself to a plate of rashers and eggs before seating himself across from her. "Do you have a busy day ahead?"

She lowered the tabloid paper she was perusing. "The usual. Louisa has agreed to accompany me on some of my morning calls. And we will pick up some items in town. Then there is the Johnson dinner this evening. I hope you will join us."

"Not tonight, Mother. I have other plans." In truth, he would *find* other plans. He had no intention of subjecting himself to an entire evening making polite conversation with Lady Johnson and her daughter. "Please convey my regrets."

His mother gave an almost inaudible huff and eased her paper up, but she offered no protest. "I was hoping you could accompany your sister and me to the theater two nights hence. Would that be possible?"

"I don't see why not. I enjoy the theater." He had hoped the Burleson event had satisfied her matchmaking efforts for the week, at least, but it was not to be.

"Will you be seeing Viscount Montgomery today?" she asked, feigning nonchalance.

"Yes. We have plans to meet up later," Alex said, shaking open the newspaper Hartford, the butler, had laid out for him. "I won't be home for dinner tonight, Mother."

"Louisa and I may have an early dinner. I'll see what she prefers." She took a bite of her toast. "Do you plan to return to that gambling den?"

Alex bit his tongue. "We plan to eat at Dolly's Chop House this evening. It's been a long time since I've been there."

"Excellent food. Your father and I used to eat there occasionally."

"I didn't realize that, Mother."

"Indeed. There are probably a few things you don't realize about me," she retorted with a sly smile. "Please give my regards to Lord Montgomery. Let him know he is mentioned in this morning's *Morning Post*." With that, she stood. "Alex, I have been searching for something of your father's and have not been able to locate it."

An icy chill crept down his spine. Was she getting ready to ask about the townhouse? What would he say?

"Your father kept a diary from the time we courted. I have missed him terribly, and the diaries have provided succor." She blushed. "When we courted, he frequently wrote of his feelings. Reading through his thoughts has stirred memories and has been a tremendous comfort. He would not have simply stopped writing. It was something he did every day. The last one I found had an entry a year before his death." She shook her head slowly and sighed. "Should you find anything out of place in the study, it was probably me. I have searched every book on the shelf, to no advantage. It would mean a lot to me to find it." She swiped at the sudden tears that tumbled from her eyes.

"Mother, I had no idea Father kept a diary. He never once mentioned it to me." How had he never known this? A diary could detail his sudden... madness. It could be a tremendous help.

"There are many things parents don't tell their children, simply because there is no need."

"I shall make every effort to find it for you, Mother."

She walked over to him, put both hands to his face, and looked into his eyes. "You are a good son, Alex," she said, before exiting the breakfast room.

When the door closed behind her, Alex mindlessly picked up the paper she had been reading, recalling her comment about Montgomery's name. He spotted it at the top of the second page. It read:

> *It is rumored that a certain Lord SM was entered into the betting book at White's following Lord and Lady Burleson's event. This writer wonders which of the Albertine twin ladies caught his notice. Could the self-avowed bachelor be planning to wed?*

"Blast!" Alex said, closing the paper. Montgomery would not be pleased. He could only imagine that Lady Albertine fed this morsel to the gossip rag. *Odious woman.* He finished his rashers and washed them down with his hot tea. "It'll be the last time I'm able to drag him with me to one of Mother's ridiculous events."

He would tackle the problem this afternoon. For now, he needed to focus on how to tell Lord Burleson what his daughter was doing. As he opened the door, he almost ran into the butler holding his salver.

"Lord Wrotham, you have a caller," Hartford said, extending the salver.

Alex picked up the card and flipped it over.

> *Mr. Robert Bennett*
> *Bow Street*

Great timing! "Is he in my study?"

"He is, my lord."

Alex would have more answers before meeting up with Montgomery. "Have a footman visit Lord Burleson and ask him if he can see me." He didn't want to risk Burleson's not being there. Alex walked with Hartford in the direction of his study. "Let Williams know I'll be later leaving than I anticipated—probably thirty minutes."

"I will see it is done, my lord," the burly retainer said, with a bow, before removing himself.

Alex arrived at his study and found Bennett standing beside his father's desk, gazing down at it with a wrinkled brow. "Is something wrong with it… the desk?" Alex asked.

"No, my lord. Quite the opposite. I haven't seen this model of desk since I was a boy. My grandfather owned one. Grandpapa's desk had several secret storage places in which my brother and I would hide notes and hand-drawn treasure maps, pretending we were spies trying to save the country." Bennett shook his head. "I apologize. The sight of it simply took me back. I lost my brother in the war. And those were good memories."

"Your grandfather was a barrister, if I recall correctly, known for both his cleverness and his fairness. My grandfather employed him."

Alex viewed his father's heavy cherry desk as if seeing it for the first time. It was one he, too, had inherited from his grandfather, although there had been no mention of any secret drawers. *Interesting.*

"Can I offer you refreshments?" he asked, taking a seat behind the desk and gesturing for Bennett to follow.

"Thank you, but no. I just left a filling breakfast with my family," Bennett said, giving a playful pat to his sizeable belly. "I've several things to tell you, my lord. First, we investigated Mrs. Marble. The woman had an illustrious past—before she became part of the theater. She grew up in a bordello near Covent Gardens, run by her aunt. Her mother was not a prostitute, but reportedly Marble was born on the wrong side of the blanket. Her father was a peer."

"Interesting... Marble is a by-blow of a member of the peerage. That could be part of what motivates her," Alex mumbled.

"I hadn't thought of that, but yes, that could be her incitement. Here's where it gets interesting. Marble has a close relationship with Lord Anders and has for many years."

"His mistress?"

"At first, I thought so. But I'm not sure. And we've watched her apartment. He leaves before dark when he visits her townhouse."

Alex scowled at the reference to the townhouse he was sure was stolen—he just didn't know how.

"We aren't sure," Bennett continued. "They don't appear to even like each other when they are together."

"Then what?"

"I don't have anything that I can prove, but I suspect there is a different connection between the two of them," Bennett said. "She had been entertaining Anders when I met with her. Anders had just left. Maddeningly, the woman denied knowing anything about robbing your carriage." He withdrew a stubby pencil and flipped open his pad, checking off an item. "I met with Mrs. Dove-Lyon. As you indicated, she paid a visit to ensure the two men found their way to the Old Bailey for what they had done. I expect that to occur soon—or at least a transfer to Newgate while they await trial."

"Did she mention anything about Anders?" Alex asked.

He looked up and smiled. "That's on my list. As you know, her husband and your father were best friends—while Anders and your father were distant cousins. Third cousins, if I have it right. She recalled it because, according to her late husband, your father never had the time of day for Anders. But she told me something I found interesting. She overheard a conversation suggesting your father had joined Anders in some sort of business venture. She only mentioned it as an off-hand thing, but I sensed she dropped it deliberately."

"Interesting. Perhaps my mother can shed light on the relationship. I cannot recall it ever being mentioned. And I'm almost certain Mother knows nothing of any business venture with Anders. She told me everything she thought Father had been involved with before he became ill. This is a complete surprise." Alex scrunched up his brow thoughtfully. "I should visit my solicitor as soon as possible to clarify this."

"Good. Will you let me know what you find out?" Bennett asked as he entered another checkmark on his pad.

"Yes. It could be important."

The detective scribbled a note. "I make lists because I become so easily enthused with aspects of my job that I sometimes forget to mention something." He lightly tapped the pad against his leg. "This keeps me straight." He chortled.

Alex smiled. "I find myself making lists these days." He planned to add *this* to his list.

Bennett cleared his throat. "Now, this is purely an observation. When I asked Mrs. Marble if she had any connection to the robbery attempt, I would swear her initial reaction was one of surprise. She quickly schooled her face to appear in control. But I detected irritation when I mentioned one of the men let slip she was involved. It was her look of surprise that seemed off."

"She *is* an actress," Alex observed.

"Yes. True. But still, I found her initial surprise somewhat remarkable. What's more is, when I asked her about the ownership of the townhouse and her relationship with your father, she turned coy and pulled out the deed, handing it to me. It showed both his acquisition of it and where he signed it over to her. If I had a reason to believe it wasn't his signature, I could have taken the deed and had it examined. I recommend you speak with your father's solicitor."

"Yes, I already have a meeting set. You've given me some good information." It was disturbing information, but Alex hoped it would lead him to answers. "Do you have anything else?"

"Yes. One more observation. It has to do with the taller of the two men we are holding, Jerome Butler. When I asked him if he knew Marble, he quickly said no, but it was clear he was lying. And he refuses to tell anything about the relationship. But when I asked about Anders, he appeared scared, and said he didn't know him." He shrugged. "Just seems worth noting."

"Indeed. I agree." There had been several times in the past few years with Wellington where recognizing subtle inconsistencies had solved problems. "I will get back to you after I speak with my mother and our solicitors."

Bennett nodded and stood. "I'll take my leave."

Alex opened the door to find Hartford walking up. "Hartford. Mr. Bennett was just leaving."

"I will escort him to the door, my lord," the butler said, giving a short bow before showing the detective out.

Minutes later, the retainer returned. "I didn't want to share your business with your guest, my lord. The footman delivered your message and said you would be expected. And Williams just pulled up with your carriage, my lord."

Alex had become so absorbed in Bennett's information that he nearly forgot about his trip to the Burlesons'. Grabbing his greatcoat, hat, and cane, he hurried to the waiting carriage.

Chapter Nine

Burleson House

"It's very good to see you, Lord Wrotham. Please follow me. Lord Burleson is in his study and is expecting you."

"Thank you, Arlington," Alex said, handing the butler his greatcoat, cane, and hat.

As he entered the study, Lord Burleson rose to greet him. "May I offer you some refreshments, Wrotham?"

"Yes, I would appreciate something to drink." Alex noticed the brandy on Burleson's desk. "I'll have a brandy, if that's what you're having."

"Certainly. That will be all, Arlington."

"Very good, my lord," the retainer said, giving a short bow before leaving.

Alex took a seat while Burleson poured brandy into a crystal glass and handed it to him. "This particular brandy is my favorite," the earl said.

Alex swirled it in the cup and took a sip, enjoying the warmth. "It is French, is it not? I agree—it's a solid choice."

"I confess, I was most interested to find out why you needed to see me so urgently," Burleson said.

Alex took a sip of the brandy and bought himself a moment to decide how best to broach the subject of the man's errant daughter. He took a deep breath and let it out slowly. "What I'm about to say may shock you, but I feel it needs to be said. Lady Priscilla has been dressing as a man and playing cards at the Lyon's Den. I have seen her twice. The first time, I didn't recognize her. The second time, I thought I recognized her... and I followed her when she left. She entered your house. It was your daughter. I am certain."

The man's face went ashen, but only for the slightest moment, before his color returned. He closed his eyes and took a breath. "Her mother will be most displeased with me for teaching her cards." Opening his eyes, Burleson studied Alex for a moment. "She is winning, I assume."

Alex chuckled, despite himself. "Oh yes! She has an excellent record of wins." He glanced around the room. "I cannot imagine what she needs the money for, but she has won quite handily."

"You said you recognized her. How?"

Alex bit the inside of his cheek to not smile. "Part of her disguise involves muttonchops, a mustache, and a brown wig. The sideburns are too bushy for the young man she portrays—forcing one to look closer at Mr. Paul Smith. I found this happening the first time I saw her in the den. When I looked closer, I could see a mole near her ear, although I couldn't see the distinctive shape of the mole. When we visited for the party, I noticed she had a heart-shaped mole in the same place Mr. Smith's was. She is confident and has a flair for card playing. Finally, Mr. Smith had the hackney drop her off at the Millers' residence, next door to your townhouse, where she walked with a young girl of about ten and her dog—both of whom she rescued from some unruly boys who were punishing them with rocks on the way home from the Lyon's Den. I watched them make their way to your townhouse—it looked like they used the servants' entrance. Unless you have a young man by the name of Paul Smith living here, *he* is your daughter."

Wide-eyed, Burleson leaned back in his chair. After a moment, he leaned forward. "You say she brought a child and a dog home with her... *yesterday*? How have I seen no evidence of"—he waved his hand—*"this?"*

"Do you have a man in service about her size?"

"My valet," he murmured, almost to himself. "How can this be true?"

As if in answer to his question, a dog barked. It sounded like it was coming from the back of the house.

Startled, both men sat ramrod straight, glanced at the door, and then back at each other.

Alex bit his other cheek to quash his impulse to laugh. He wished he could be a fly on the wall when Lady Priscilla explained the child and dog. As comical as it all seemed, his main concern was her well-being. Lord and Lady Burleson knew nothing of their eldest daughter's shenanigans. Alex was tempted to ask how she had managed to hide the child and dog, but he refrained. "I am concerned for her safety, Burleson," he said instead.

"As am I," the man said hoarsely. "The girl has always had a mind of her own. Pianofortes, sewing, and painting were nothing that interested her. She excelled in studies, mastering languages, and anything else the governess threw at her. Once she learned mathematics, she pursued whatever applications of it she could. I taught her chess and cards—and she took to cards like a fish to water. Her skill surpasses my own." He buried his head in his hands for a few moments before looking up. "I know my daughter. Before I can stop her, I must find out *why* she is doing this and, at the same time, protect her. Otherwise, she will find another way to achieve whatever goal she has that inspired this." Despairing, he scrubbed his face with his hands.

"You must help me!"

"Me?" Alex's voice rose.

"Yes! Of course. This could work," Burleson said, standing and pacing behind his desk. "And the sooner we start, the better." The earl stopped pacing and regarded Alex. "I would be in your debt if you would help me. You already have unmasked her, so to speak. That would allow me to speak with Mrs. Dove-Lyon, and possibly uncover what is motivating her."

Alex started to suggest Burleson could lock the girl in her room, but cooled on the idea as soon as he thought it. *This could work in my favor.* "If I consent to 'court' her—because that is what people will think when they see us together—we must both agree it is not to woo her and there would be no obligation to marry."

Burleson arched a brow and studied Alex. "My alternative would be to have a footman follow her everywhere, and a guard to watch our house. Priscilla would see through that in no time. It would be for a short time until I could get to the bottom of this. And I agree to those terms."

"How would we handle her gaming as Mr. Smith?" Alex asked.

Her father gave that some thought. "I can see no other way but to have you out her—but in private to her. Threaten to tell me about it if she doesn't consent to your escort whenever she goes to the den. She will bow her back, but she has no room to negotiate."

Alex nodded. That made sense. "And what about the courting? I hate to lead her to the wrong conclusion."

Lord Burleson grimaced. "Let it start innocently enough—perhaps a couple of outings. I expect to get to the bottom of this quickly. I will meet with Mrs. Dove-Lyon. If I know my daughter, she has been worrying about the dog and child and will approach me about those two before long. She doesn't like surprises and will want to control the situation." He shook his head. "I have never seen her display this type of behavior. My wife will blame me if she finds out because she told me not to teach her so many card games. Of course, that made Priscilla want to learn them more."

The poor man was in over his head with this daughter, Alex feared. But he could not deny an attraction to the young woman. This arrangement would allow him to get to know her, without the threat of marriage hanging over his head. Only a fool would walk away from this arrangement. *And I am no fool.*

"My wife told me you danced with Priscilla a couple of times at the party—waltzes, I believe. I assume there is an attraction on your part." Burleson arched a brow and seemed to wait for Alex to answer. When Alex said nothing, Burleson sighed in resignation and continued. "I can see your reputation as a good card player is well earned, Wrotham. I will agree to your terms—but you must agree to mine. But… if you ruin my daughter, you will marry her."

"I do not ruin innocents, sir," Alex returned. "Your terms are agreeable. My mother mentioned wanting to go to the theater in two days. If you are amenable, I will ask your daughter to join us."

"We are in total agreement. My wife will be thrilled. I'm not ready to share our arrangement with her—at least not until I get a better handle on my daughter's motivation."

Alex took a final sip of his brandy. "Agreed. I will take good care of her, Lord Burleson." He stood and shook the man's hand. "If you do not object, I should like to ask Lady Priscilla before I leave. She may assume I met with you to ask permission to court her."

"Excellent!" Relief showed on the man's face. "Sterling idea. The sooner this gets started, the better. I don't want to think of her without a protector. And I promise to rectify this as soon as possible." Without waiting for a response, Burleson rang for Arlington, who quickly appeared.

"My lord, your daughters wish to meet with you," the butler intoned.

Alex and Burleson looked at each other with raised brows.

"Let Lady Priscilla and Lady Jane know I will be happy to meet with them *soon*." He emphasized the last word. "Lord Wrotham wishes to see Lady Priscilla first. Direct him to the parlor and ask Mary to join her as a chaperone."

"Yes, my lord. Lord Wrotham, I will take you to the parlor and ask Lady Priscilla to join you," Arlington said.

Alex thanked Lord Burleson and followed the retainer.

The butler opened a glass-paned door leading into the parlor. The room was bright and had a comfortable feel. Blue damask curtains framed a large window that opened to the front of the house, where red and white Lenten roses, all dappled with rich maroon, extended the length of the black iron fencing that surrounded the five-storied townhouse. His mother often commented on the beauty of Lenten roses, claiming the flower as one of her favorites. Blue floral Aubusson carpet and a white-and-gold-striped damask settee dominated the room.

"You asked to see me?" Lady Priscilla asked, walking into the parlor.

He turned and noted her hands clutched the sides of a pale blue shawl, draped loosely about her shoulders. She nodded to her maid, who took a seat across the room near the large secretary desk.

Smiling, Alex extended his leg and gave an elegant bow. "Good afternoon, Lady Priscilla. I stopped by on a mission." At least that was true. He had been on a mission. "Shall we be comfortable and sit?"

"Yes, of course," she said, taking a seat at the far end of the settee.

He chose the yellow-and-blue-upholstered chair angled next to the sofa, nearest to her. "I suppose I should apologize. I didn't think of flowers until I saw the gorgeous garden in front of your home and realized I had come empty handed."

She blushed.

Not wanting her to be uncomfortable, he continued. "I would be honored if you would attend the theater with my family two evenings from now. My mother and sister will be in attendance, so you will be well chaperoned."

Lady Priscilla opened her mouth to speak, then closed it before finally responding. "This is so unexpected, Lord Wrotham. I-I would be thrilled, my lord. *Romeo and Juliet* is playing! I never dreamed to go to this production. It's one of my favorite Shakespeare stories." Delight ran warm in her voice.

"You like the Bard?" he said, enthralled by her exuberance. "I confess, I try to see all of his plays."

Her lavender eyes brightened. "I *love* the theater, and Shakespeare is my favorite playwright. It will be my pleasure to join you and your family."

At least they had this in common. It would make the outing that much more delightful. He gazed at Lady Priscilla in the white muslin day dress with the blue shawl and noticed she had relaxed considerably in the last few minutes. Alex observed the maid kept her head down, and her hands folded, no doubt listening to every word. There was nothing to be done about that. "Excellent! Then it is settled. My family and I will pick you up at seven on Thursday evening."

Priscilla stood and held out her gloved hand.

Alex lifted her hand and leaned over to kiss it. "Until Thursday." For a moment their gazes locked, and he couldn't help but notice how beautiful she was with loose auburn curls framing her face.

Her cheeks pinked. "Until Thursday, my lord."

Alex pulled out his pocket watch and checked the time. *Perfect. I have just enough time to get to Gentleman Jackson's,* he thought. After the day he had already put in, he could use the workout.

Chapter Ten

That morning, Priscilla and Jane had agreed on a story regarding Maggie and Penny. Priscilla was on her way to her father's study when she heard male voices—her father's and... *his*.

Lord Alex Wrotham's presence still unnerved her. It made her feel things she wasn't used to feeling... like the need to be kissed. Without thinking, she ducked into a nearby closet. She heard her father offer refreshments and close the door. The back of her neck prickled.

She had debated hiding behind the abnormally large potted tree outside of her father's study to listen. It had been strategically placed to absorb the morning sunlight from the large window on the opposite wall. But when Arlington's slow and steady footsteps passed outside of the door to the closet, she abandoned that approach. The butler watched Papa's study door like a hawk, often seeming to magically appear as her father opened the door to dismiss a visitor. Espionage conducted from behind a potted plant would have been a horrible idea, she thought, grateful she hadn't followed the impulse.

Hoping she could make the steps before the door opened, she slowly reemerged and sprinted toward the stairs, taking them two at a time until she reached the second landing. Leaning over, she caught her breath, then made her way to her room.

"What took you so long? Was Papa angry?" Jane asked.

"Please, one question at a time," Priscilla huffed, still trying to catch her breath from her sprint up the stairs. She drew a deep breath and let it out slowly to calm herself. When she felt better, she faced her sister. "I fear this has become a large muddle. I left Maggie in the kitchen with her dog. Cook is not pleased about the dog being inside, but had she not fed the dog in the kitchen to begin with, the dog may have remained outside," she stated flatly. "I believe she, too, has become smitten with the child and her dog, as has the rest of the staff. I've heard Arlington saw Penny but did not order the animal out. He saved his table scraps for her."

The sisters snickered.

"If we are not careful, the raggedy dog will become massive," Jane suggested. "With that long body and short, thick legs, she's positively precious!"

"And remarkably smart! Rose will adore her. Fortunately, her governess is keeping her busy in the nursery today," Priscilla added. "Our biggest problem is Mama. She visits the kitchen each day. I am holding my breath, expecting a loud shriek at any time. And I didn't get to see Papa. We should do that as soon as possible."

"You're right. We must smooth this out with Papa before it becomes more of a tangle," Jane agreed.

On their way to their father's study, Priscilla and Jane ran into their mother, who approached from the direction of the kitchen.

"My dears! What you both did was so charitable! I cannot imagine the horror of seeing a dog and child maimed. What is this city coming to? We must have Dr. Spencer examine the child. I would make sure we do all that we can for her. Perhaps we can place her near Rose once we are certain of her health. They are both ten and would likely enjoy each other's company. And her dog—she is just the sweetest!"

Was their mother *gushing*?

"M-Mama! I realize this is all a huge surprise. I had hoped to..." Priscilla started.

"Pish! I understand you and Jane had little choice but to bring the child home. I declare, she looks like a picture I've seen. Pity I cannot put my finger on it, but it will come to me. Have you spoken with your father?"

"No, that was where we are heading," Jane replied.

"I will join you there shortly."

Priscilla had no notion of what to think—and right now, she didn't have time to think about it. But this was the first time in memory that her mother had become her champion. She wasn't sure why—or what Cook and Maggie had told her—but she remained silent. It was always best to let others speak first. That was her mother's rule, and for once, she would follow it.

Priscilla opened the door to their father's study, where he stood with his back to them, looking out the window behind his desk. He turned and smiled, indicating with a nod the chairs in front of his desk. "Girls! Do have a seat."

"How are you today, Papa?" Priscilla asked as she took a seat. She regarded her sister before speaking again. "Jane and I have a particular matter to discuss."

"How did your meeting with Wrotham go, daughter?" he asked.

Priscilla studied her father's face, but he gave no indication he knew anything. "Lord Wrotham asked me to go to the theater with him on Thursday evening."

"The theater in two days. We—your mother and I—would have no objection to that. How do you feel about it?" he asked.

Priscilla did her best to maintain a sedate appearance, while at the same time still the butterflies that were swirling excitedly in her stomach from the kiss he had given her hand only ten minutes ago. "I'm not sure. It was a surprise." *More like a shock!* Just his kiss on the back of her hand had tilted her world completely, sending her thoughts spiraling back through the dreams she had had these last few days. *What would his kiss taste like on my lips?* "I had no expectations of meeting with him."

"Even though he danced twice with you at the ball?" Her father waggled his eyebrows.

Her face heated. "Papa! He was probably doing what his mother had requested of him."

"Bah! I have never known red-blooded Englishmen to kowtow to their mother's dance choices."

"The countess can be quite formidable," she insisted.

"Wrotham's an earl. Don't be ridiculous. The man would not have asked you to dance, or to the theater, had there not been some level of interest," her father replied.

Priscilla wanted to ask what he had been speaking to Lord Wrotham about earlier. But her father was not one to divulge business or confidences.

"What was it you wanted to speak with me about?" he asked, pouring himself a drink, with his back turned to her. Turning back, he nodded toward a serving cart. "Would you care for some refreshment? Arlington brought some lemonade and biscuits earlier. I thought I wanted them but found my appetite had left me. They've barely been touched."

"A cup of lemonade would be nice." Priscilla was thankful for the extra minutes.

"Papa, I would love a glass of lemonade," Jane said. "And are those Cook's lemon biscuits? May I have one?"

"Jane! They are, and you may," he replied with a hearty laugh. "This must be an important meeting, because the two of you are acting very formal." He handed Jane and Priscilla glasses of lemonade. Jane took a few biscuits before taking a seat.

Jane offered her sister a biscuit, but Priscilla waved it off. If things didn't go as she hoped, the last thing she wanted was food in her stomach.

Taking a seat behind his desk, the earl leaned back and steepled his fingers. "What is so important that my girls requested a special meeting? Why not tell me at breakfast?"

The girls glanced at one another. "I have done something…" Priscilla began.

"As have I," interjected Jane, giving her sister a quelling glance. "When we went shopping yesterday for ribbons, there was a girl and her dog being maimed by boys with rocks and sticks. Priscilla and I offered her the safety of our carriage. And… we couldn't leave them, Papa!"

"What do you mean, you *couldn't leave them*?" He blinked. "They are here?"

"Yes, Papa. They are in the kitchen. Cook has been helping with them. We've already located some frocks to fit little Maggie," Jane explained.

The door to the study opened, and their mother stepped inside. "Oh, darlings, you hadn't exaggerated at all. They need all the help we can give them. I've already contacted Dr. Spencer," she said, looking meaningfully at her daughters. "I can attest to what they've told you." She looked at her husband. "We have very generous daughters, darling." With that, the countess stepped out. Before she shut the door, they could hear her say, "Please fill a tub with warm water to wash Penny. Girls, please join me a little later so we can make some plans."

Priscilla looked at Jane, who gave the tiniest of shrugs. "Of course, Mama," they chimed in together.

Lord Burleson scratched his head for a second. "Since your mother supports their stay, I suppose I have nothing else to add. She will make sure all that is needed is done." He took a deep breath. "Will there be anything else?" he said on an exhale, giving a lingering look in Priscilla's direction, as if he wanted to say something more.

"No, Papa." She stood. "Thank you for your understanding..."

"And support," Jane added.

"If that will be all, I will be going out for a few hours, girls," Lord Burleson said, rising from behind his desk.

And just like that, the meeting Priscilla had dreaded was over, but what had just happened? *Nothing about this day seemed ordinary.*

She had just been asked to visit the theater with Lord Wrotham and his family two nights from now. Her heart galloped at the thought. Lord Wrotham's very nearness sent her pulse into flutters. When she had walked into the room, she had fully expected to gain her father's support by pulling on familiar heartstrings. Never in her wildest dreams did she expect her mother—without prompting—to wholeheartedly offer her support.

Priscilla puzzled over the events of the morning as she and Jane climbed the stairs to her room.

A scratch sounded at the door. Priscilla and Jane glanced at each other before Priscilla said, "Come in."

A maid walked in with a small tray of refreshments. "Your mother requested I bring this for you, my ladies," the young girl said.

"Thank you, Joanna," Priscilla said, glancing at her sister. "It's so unexpected."

"It is!" her mother said, swishing into the room. "But then, it's impossible to make sense of everything all the time."

"Who are you, and what have you done with my mother?" Priscilla asked good-humoredly.

Mama smiled. "Sometimes, one needs to *trust* their daughters, especially when they have been kind. And I do... trust my daughters." She gave a fond look at both. "I just met the little girl, Maggie. Simply a charming child." The countess tapped her chin with her forefinger. "She reminds me of someone, but I'm unable to recall whom just now. But I sent word earlier for Dr. Spencer to visit us. I expect him this afternoon. Penny appears healthy, but one never knows. It's best to check and do what is necessary. Cook explained that you ladies rescued the child on your way home from town. How fortunate. I cannot wait to hear more about it."

Mama was onto their ruse. Had she somehow overheard them? And if so, how much?

Priscilla gave a forced smile, hoping not to react to the chills taking over her spine.

"Cilla, I recall Mama telling me about a dog you once had as a child," Jane said. "Mama once had a black dog named Penny. Does this dog resemble your childhood pet, Mama?"

"She does!" her mother answered gleefully. "My Penny was a scrappy young dog that I found stuck in a trap. Had my brother not been with me, we might never have been able to save her leg. But he managed to open the jaws of the trap and free her."

"That makes sense," Priscilla murmured.

"Yes!" Mama clasped her hands to her chest. "My mother asked no questions when we brought Penny home. In time, I discovered that dogs and cats love without reservation, and they deserve to be treated decently by people." She gave a meaningful smile. "Now, we will need to discuss the little girl, Maggie. I understand from Cook that her mother passed a month ago from consumption. Maggie affirmed that when I spoke with her. I've asked Mary to ensure the child's room is cleaned. For the time being, we shall allow her to sleep in her room on the upper floor with the servants. However, I intend to launch a search for any living relatives she may have. I could swear I've seen her resemblance… somewhere." She shook her head.

"That sounds fair, Mama. Maggie would be happy to help in the household. She only wants a safe room over her and Penny's heads. The dog insists on being near her," Priscilla explained.

"I understand, and if she is taken outside in the back of the house every few hours, I can consent to that. Maggie will be expected to take care of her animal. Apparently, our staff has taken to Penny and want to help, but they have their duties." Mama took the upholstered seat in front of Priscilla's fireplace. "We should discuss Lord Wrotham's visit. What did he wish to see you about, dear?"

"Mother, I'm sure you've already gotten the story from Mary. But he asked me to the theater with his family on Thursday evening."

Mother clasped her hands and smiled. "I'm afraid I forced her to tell. But this is all very exciting! Perhaps we can have that beautiful confection you weren't able to wear at the ball ready for you to wear."

Priscilla's eyes rounded in alarm. *Oh no!* She couldn't wear that. But how could she openly rebel after all that Mama had just done for her?

"Mary tells me that she has removed chocolate from silk before." The countess gave a small laugh. "We will make sure you don't have chocolate to drink before you leave for the theater."

"Mama, after seeing Cilla in the deeper green the other night, I realized how certain colors flatter her hair coloring—while others are more flattering for darker hair, such as yours and mine," Jane offered.

Two years separated Priscilla in age from her sister. But she quickly realized she had not given Jane her due. Her sister had matured without her notice, and related to their mother in ways Priscilla couldn't.

The countess's brow furrowed. "You could have a point, daughter," she replied. "I would like to see that Penny is properly bathed. But we should talk more about this. Perhaps there would be a more... *flattering* color for the theater."

Priscilla heard it but wasn't convinced. Her mother never wavered in getting her way, especially when the object was to control her daughters. While she had warmed to Penny and Maggie, she would not count on her to back off the orange dress. It was her favorite color, after all.

"Dr. Spencer should be here soon, and we will sort the rest of it later." With that, the countess left the room.

"Lord Burleson, I have been expecting you," Mrs. Dove-Lyon said without artifice, adjusting herself on the red velvet settee adjacent to her guest, who sat in a matching velvet chair. "I had hoped to spare you this trip, but after meeting with Lord Wrotham yesterday, I anticipated seeing you here."

"Mrs. Lyon—"

"Please. You were my husband's closest friend. I would like to think we are also friends. Call me Bessie." Her tight, red-lipped smile peeked from beneath the black veil.

Her audacity irritated him, but he chose to ignore it. "Bessie," he said. "I would offer for you to call me by my first name, Rudolph, but only my wife does that, and it's usually not at my best moments. My friends call me Burleson." He hated his first name. "Please tell me Wrotham was wrong about Mr. Paul Smith."

"Burleson. I like it," she said, not answering the question. Instead, the widow picked up a small bell and rang it. Behind him, the door opened, and an Asian woman walked in carrying a silver tray with a hot pot of tea and placed it between them on a silver cart. The woman gave a slight nod and left the room.

"Tea?" the widow asked.

"Thank you, yes," Burleson managed, accepting the proffered cup. "You didn't answer my question, but I assume your non-answer was the answer."

"Yes," she replied matter-of-factly. "Your daughter and Mr. Paul Smith are the same." She sipped her tea. "When your daughter approached me with this harebrained idea, she told me she planned to accumulate wealth so that she could establish her own home, independent of her family." She paused and took a cleansing breath.

"The easiest way to do this is to say it. Your wife smothers her and makes all her choices—including how she presents to the *ton*. She forces her to sing, when she can't sing, because she cannot play the pianoforte."

"Priscilla never cared for the instrument," Burleson murmured.

"Yes. Your daughter mentioned that. She feels that, at eighteen years of age, having never been courted, her chances of finding a husband, and that traditional avenue of independence, are slim. People mock her. Within earshot, they laugh at her. She has a stutter that she cannot control when she is uncomfortable."

"She told you all of this," he said incredulously. It was a statement, not a question. Burleson's grip on the thin porcelain teacup tightened, so he shakily returned it to the dish.

Bessie did not reply immediately. Instead, she took another sip of tea. "I tried to deny your daughter. To my utter shock, she threatened that if I didn't go along with it, she would pursue her goals elsewhere. Of course, I tested her talent—which is considerable—with my dealer and one other trusted associate. She attributes her skill to you, saying it has always been a connection between you two."

"It has. She has a mind for puzzles and numbers, but no interest in the typical female pursuits. I thought games would be perfect for her, and she took to it like a fish to water." He ran his hand through his hair and muttered, "Perhaps Milly—my wife—was right."

Bessie airily swept a hand around the room and gave a throaty laugh. "You believe a woman cannot choose smarter hobbies like chess and cards over being humiliated singing out of tune in front of a supercilious group of men and women?" Her voice dripped with sarcasm. "You would be wrong. As a consideration to my former husband's friendship with you, my lord, I agreed to her demands, but with compromises. Your daughter—portraying Mr. Smith—arrives at the side door in a hack and is shown to a table. While she can play anyone she wishes, they must approach her. I do not allow her to mingle. When she cashes out, Titan sees she is placed in a waiting hackney. The driver is given specific instructions to drop her off near her home."

Relief washed over him. "Lord Wrotham brought this to me, concerned for her safety."

A smile flickered on her lips. "I see."

"He agreed to help me by keeping her busy, and therefore out of trouble. The man is doing this as a favor to me until I can resolve this situation."

"I see you are not to be underestimated, my friend. Lord Wrotham is a very sought-after young man, but protests he has no interest in marrying," she began. "Many of the *ton*'s marriage-minded mammas would give their eyeteeth to have the handsome earl chaperoning their daughters—your wife included, I suspect."

"While I had noticed an attraction, there had been no intended manipulation… not initially." A smile tugged at the corner of his mouth.

"Ah. I see. Lord Wrotham is a very canny card player himself, yet in this, you have outplayed him." She snorted. "So, he is courting her—sort of—but as a favor. Wrotham wouldn't have agreed to your request if he had no interest. My husband always regarded you as cunning." She paused. "I assure you, my people remain as vigilant as possible whenever she comes."

"Your reputation for making unusual matches precedes you. My wife has mentioned it on more than one occasion."

"Yes. It is deserved," she said. "It is a means of income for me, and a sought-after remedy for the women whose daughters find themselves in difficult positions, and it is easily supported by my business."

"I plan to discuss this with my daughter. To hear that she wishes to live apart from her family cuts to the bone, and I must know *why*." Just saying it put a lump in his throat. Priscilla had always been his pride and joy. Yet he had not stood up to his wife and her crazy notions—

the colors, the weird feathers in the girls' hair. The exhibitions. Guilt coursed through him. He would speak to his wife immediately.

"But since you will have her well chaperoned, let us allow this to play out a little longer," Bessie suggested. "We should give the earl and your daughter some time together—just to see where it goes."

"You are suggesting…"

"Exactly—a match. These arrangements rarely fail, and I must confess, the idea of this match…" She hesitated. "I have a feeling about these two."

The earl considered her suggestion. "Wrotham doesn't plan for this to last long."

"We'll see," she said. "Lord Alex Wrotham may be a wonderful foil to your daughter's mischief."

Burleson couldn't stop the smile that emerged. "Your idea has merit, but I'm not sure it will work."

"Lord Burleson, I have seen matches made that even I gave little chance of succeeding. Let's give it a little air to breathe."

Burleson gave a respectful nod. "My main concern is her safety. Thank you for your hospitality and the information, Bessie. I will bid you a good day."

"Your coach will be waiting at the side of the building. I'll have Titan show you out the private entrance to assure privacy."

A black, unmarked carriage passed as Lord Burleson exited the Lyon's Den and entered his awaiting conveyance.

Chapter Eleven

The next day

ALEX STEPPED FROM his carriage on Broad Street and stared up at the five-storied building housing his father's solicitor's office. "I shouldn't be long, Williams," he said, adjusting his hat and tapping the conveyance door closed with his cane.

"Yes, my lord," Williams said. "I will be here when you leave."

The man had done an admirable job filling in as a driver, but Alex was glad Strafford was seeing Dr. Spencer today. Hopefully, the doctor would release him so he could come back to the job tomorrow.

Stepping inside the gray stone building in front of him, Alex climbed the stairs to the second floor, stopping in front of his father's solicitor's office. A bell jingled when he opened the door.

"Good morning, Lord Wrotham," the thin, bespectacled man said, not moving from the desk that stood sentry in front of a short hallway. "Mr. Adams is expecting you."

"Thank you, Saunders."

A minute later, the door to the office opened and a short, balding man stepped back from the door. "I thought I heard your voice. It's very good to see you again, Lord Wrotham," Adams said, giving a brief nod before waving him into his office. "Please make yourself comfortable." He turned to his assistant. "Thank you, Saunders."

"I'll get right to the point," Alex said in the office. "My father supposedly gave away a Mayfair property to a Mrs. Marble. I would like to know what you know about it."

"I'm pretty sure that couldn't have happened—at least not the way Mrs. Marble is claiming. Give me a minute," the man said, adjusting his glasses. He looked in a ledger book, and then called out to Saunders.

"Yes, sir?"

"Saunders, pull the boxed file for the *former* Lord Wrotham."

"I anticipated you would need it, sir. Here it is," Saunders said, handing Adams a red leather box with files marked *Wrotham*.

"Good man. Thank you," Adams said, thumbing through the box's tabs. "Ah. Here it is." He pulled the document out gently. "We had a scribe who no longer works here and who mislaid some of your father's file—or I would have given you a copy of this on your initial visit." He handed a duplicate, marked *copy*, to Alex. "This is the deed for the townhouse."

Alex scanned the deed. "Father signed the townhouse over to me almost two years before he died."

"Yes, that is a copy of the deed that was registered. I daresay her copy has not been registered, as it would have been recognized by the Land Registry as a forgery."

Alex smiled. "I've got her!" he murmured to himself.

"Pardon?"

"I was saying thank you. Is this a copy I may keep?" Alex asked.

"You may. It is your copy. I always make two copies of any deed and have them signed. I keep a copy in my safe. This is a copy intended for your father. I gave it to him, but he forgot to take it with him, and I held it for him." Adams picked up the copy. "Your father transferred ownership to you, and it was recorded at the Land Registry that very day."

"And that would have been before Mrs. Marble claimed to have received the deed from my father."

"I make it a point not to disparage people, but this is not the first time I've had peers in here, looking up a deed. There have been several pieces of property purportedly inherited by Mrs. Marble," Adams said. "This was not one. Your father was a good man, and he specifically wanted you to have that property, thinking that, as a bachelor, you might want your own townhouse—one away from your parents."

"This provides proof that her document is a forgery. A fake." Alex was so relieved to find the document that emotion threatened to overwhelm him. Silently he thanked his father. "My father was thoughtful and generous with his children." Carefully, he rolled up the document and tucked it in his inside pocket. "Thank you for your time, Mr. Adams."

"You are welcome. Please… call upon us for any of your legal needs," the rotund man said as Alex left his office.

He left feeling better than he had in weeks. He finally had her!

Williams rolled up with the carriage. "Take me to White's," Alex said, closing the door and sitting down. The carriage lurched forward.

He had exactly what he needed to prove Delores Marble was not the owner of the townhouse. But after hearing his father had kept a diary, he had thought of little else but finding that diary and Lady Priscilla. He planned to look for the diary, but he wasn't sure what to do about the lady who consumed his thoughts. Her father's request that he court her had only confused things more.

"I wonder what Montgomery will have to say about Burleson's request," he mused out loud to himself. It felt like he had a muddle on his hands, although there were parts of this muddle that rather pleased him.

His carriage turned onto St. James and approached the front of White's, where it slowed to a stop. "Thank you, Williams." He stepped from the carriage and tugged his coat tighter against the cold burst of wind. "Pick me up in two hours."

"Yes, my lord." His driver nodded, and the carriage lurched forward.

A footman held the door for him as he rushed up the last few steps. "My lord, may I take your coat, hat, and cane?"

"Yes, Randolph. That suits. Have you seen Viscount Montgomery?"

"He's sitting by the fireplace in the coffee room. I believe he mentioned holding a seat for you when he entered."

"Over here, Wrotham," Montgomery yelled from across the room. He flagged down a footman that walked by. "Two brandies and a tray of meats and cheeses."

"Yes, my lord, right away," the servant replied.

"Montgomery, thank you for grabbing the warmest spot in the club! The wind outside is raw," Alex said, warming his hands over the open flames of the fireplace.

"The cold would have felt good yesterday when we left Jackson's. My bruises have bruises," Montgomery said good-naturedly.

"We haven't done that in an age. I'd gone soft. Let's do this again next week," Alex replied.

The footman brought the drinks and food and placed them between them on a wooden table.

"Put it on my tab, Roy," Alex said. He looked at his friend. "My turn. And things are looking up for me."

"Really! Tell me."

Alex patted his pocket. "I have the evidence to get her out of my townhouse."

"*Your* townhouse?"

"Yes. Father signed it over and registered the deed at least a year before he was even seen with Marble." Alex reached into his coat pocket and unfurled it, handing it to his friend. "I feel like celebrating!" He picked up his brandy glass and clinked it against his friend's before taking a sip.

"Perhaps we are celebrating too soon. Mrs. Marble still has possession of the townhouse," Montgomery pointed out.

"True," Alex said, then sipped his brandy, appreciating the burning warmth.

"I've had an interesting day, too." Montgomery laid down a slip of paper with a page number on it. "It's a bet with my name next to it in the betting book. Page five hundred and sixty-seven, about one-third of the way down the page. The Albertine twins? Who would have written that?"

Alex nearly spewed out his brandy. "I meant to mention it yesterday," he said, wiping his lips. "I read it in Mother's paper."

"Ah… the *Morning Post*. That doesn't tell me who would have placed it there."

"I'll speak with my mother and see if she has any ideas on who it was. Chances are that she will. I also need to speak with her about Anders and find out if she knows anything about his relationship with our family."

"Does he boast of one? I've never heard any details," Montgomery said, leaning back in his chair.

"He boasts of being a distant cousin of my father's. But there's more." Alex swirled his brandy, admiring the legs of the amber liquor as it slowly moved across the glass. "I spoke with Lord Burleson about his daughter and her alias." He took a slow breath, preparing himself for what he knew would come. "And he wants me to court her… anything to protect her until he can determine why she is gambling. He is afraid for her."

Montgomery's face morphed from astonishment to hilarity, and he hooted with laughter. "Well, you certainly played those cards right!

What red-blooded male wouldn't want *that* duty? You plan to court her tonight?"

"That's good. Go on! Laugh at my expense." Alex wished he felt differently, but he *wanted* to protect her. He wanted to be with her. This provided that opportunity. What man would balk at such an assignment? "And yes, as a matter of fact, tomorrow I plan to take her to the theater with my family." He looked around and noticed that all eyes were on them. "You can stop laughing now. You've officially made us a spectacle."

"I could. But every time I think about this, it becomes more amusing. Your mother will be most pleased to see you courting." Montgomery took a sip of his brandy.

Alex placed his hand over his heart, feigning a wound. "Enough, or I will up the ante on you and the Albertine twins," he said genially.

Montgomery held his hands up in mock surrender. "All right, all right."

Alex retrieved the deed from the table, rolled it up, and tucked it in his pocket. "I met with Bennett. He said he met with Delores Marble, and she flashed a copy of the deed. It showed my father's signature signing it over to her. But he had already signed the property to me—a year or more before he supposedly began seeing her. *We have her,*" Alex said with a sneer. "I will show this to Bennett, and he can move on an eviction."

"Once he proves yours is the *real* copy, we will need to find out who did the forgery. The Home Office can help there," Montgomery mused. "Once we have her copy, we can look for telltale signs of the forger."

"Bennett thinks he can require her copy if we have a compelling case—which we do. He also mentioned one other thing to me, which I found interesting. The taller of our highwaymen, Mr. Jerome Butler, was pressed for more information about his meeting with the woman—the one who told him to take whatever they found on us that night. Bennett said he wasn't very forthcoming but pressed. Butler said their meeting was in the dark, and he never saw her face. She never gave her name, and he described her voice as raspy."

"Interesting, don't you think?" Montgomery mused. "As an actress, Mrs. Marble is trained in disguise. A raspy voice should be easy for her."

"I feel a connection exists with her, but it's hard to find supportive evidence; without that, she gets remains free to continue her antics and harass unwitting victims." Alex's jaw tightened. He would use whatever means he could to stop her. As he thought about it, he suddenly recalled the missing diaries. How had he forgotten that? "My father kept a diary—and did most of his life. Mother has found immense comfort in reading them and recalling parts of their life she hadn't thought of in years. His last diary is missing."

Montgomery sat up straight. "That could hold the key to unraveling all of this. Have you done a thorough check of his study?"

Alex rubbed his hand through his hair. "I've looked places I thought he might place it and haven't found a thing, so a more thorough search is warranted. Before she mentioned it, I hadn't known he kept one. They could be extremely helpful with the properties, but I would feel like a snoop looking through more than the most recent one. It would feel like an invasion of their privacy."

"Afraid you might find some illicit writings of your parents' activities?" Montgomery waggled his brows.

"Careful." Alex reddened at the thought of reading about his parents' private life. "I might have to take you back to Gentleman Jackson's for another round," he quipped.

"Where did he keep the completed diaries?" Montgomery said, turning serious. "I tease, but this could be the smoking gun, to coin a bad metaphor."

"I will do a thorough search when I get home."

Montgomery pulled out his watch and checked the time. "Kitterman asked that I stop by the Home Office. While I'm there, I'll ask if they've discovered anything new about Marble. Your father wasn't her first target; she has done similar things to other members of the *ton*. They have been investigating her. We know your father was not her first target—there must have been others. Maybe they will have some answers. Meanwhile, Bennett should continue to keep tabs on her."

"Come by tomorrow morning and break your fast with us. We can update each other," Alex suggested. "I know you enjoy walking everywhere, but this weather is monstrously cold. Shall I drop you off?"

"You have a deal, my friend. I was going to ask," his friend said cheekily.

Retrieving their outerwear, the two men slid on their coats and gloves, bracing for the cold. When the door opened, Alex's carriage sat out the front, waiting. "Williams has been a proper substitute for Strafford. As often as Mother demands the carriage be at her beck and call, I may adapt Williams for my needs."

"Great idea. Good drivers are hard to find, Wrotham."

A few minutes later, they pulled in front of Montgomery's townhouse, and he opened the door. "Thank you, Wrotham. I'll see you in the morning."

As the carriage passed through King Street, Alex spotted a bookstore and tapped the roof with his cane. When the carriage stopped, he opened the door. "Williams, I shouldn't be too long."

Chapter Twelve

"Grandmama! How wonderful to see you." Priscilla rushed down the stairs when her grandmother arrived. Hurrying over, she kissed her cheek. "Brrr! Your cheeks are so freezing!"

"Pish! It's brisk and breezy, is all. A perfect day for shopping." The dowager countess pulled her gloved hands from her muff and handed it to Arlington. "I woke up and decided I'm in the mood to see Madame Soyeuse today. And after seeing that magnificent color on you the other night, I thought it would be fun to see what other similar colors might suit your marvelous complexion and hair."

Jane came down behind her and kissed the dowager's cheek. "Priscilla did look stunning in the green. And it brought out those enviable lavender eyes of hers!"

"Exactly!" the older woman agreed. "How long will it take you both to get ready?"

The girls looked at each other. "We're ready!" they said together.

"Fine! Where is your mama? I should invite her as well," she said, making little effort to conceal a sigh.

"Mama is in the breakfast room. We were just going to join her," Priscilla said.

"Wonderful. I could use a hot cup of tea myself before we leave," the dowager said.

The three of them entered the breakfast room, where Priscilla's parents sat at each end of the table, each reading their favorite paper.

"Good morning, Mama!" Lord Burleson said, pushing from the table and giving his mother a welcoming kiss.

Lady Burleson lowered her paper. "It's wonderful to see you, Mama. Join us, please."

Priscilla suppressed a laugh. Mama's words were welcoming, but she noticed her facial expression said otherwise. The two women had never enjoyed an easy camaraderie, but also never uttered a disparaging word about the other. Their sighs, however, spoke volumes. Grandmama was a good foil to her mother's dictates. It had been a long time since they had ventured together to the modiste.

"The girls have agreed to accompany me to the modiste this morning. I thought it would be an excellent day for a ladies' adventure. It's too sunny a day to waste, even if the air is chilled. You are welcome to join us, Mildred."

Her mother looked up and eyed both daughters. Before she could say a word, her husband spoke.

"That's an excellent idea, Mama! Priscilla is to join Lord Wrotham's family at the theater tomorrow night. Perhaps a new frock would be in order."

"She has the orange—" Lady Burleson started.

The earl interrupted. "I agree, my dear. That dress was ruined. She will need a new dress. Please allow Priscilla and Jane to pick out fabrics—the colors of their choice—and put them on my bill... and anything else they need."

His mother clasped her hands. "Mildred, will you be joining us?"

"I think I will," the countess said, setting down her paper. "And if it's all right with you, I shall include my Rose and another child that is temporarily staying with us. The girls saved a lovely young girl named

Maggie from a horrible group of boys who were throwing stones at her. The child recently lost her mother to illness and has been on her own for weeks. Dr. Spencer has declared her healthy, and while she remains with us, she will need some frocks that fit. It makes more sense to have them made than to try to remake older ones to fit her. Would you mind if she and Rose join us?"

Priscilla opened her mouth and closed it, stunned by her mother's response. She scanned the table and saw similar expressions on everyone's face, including her grandmother's. While she loved her mother, Priscilla had never seen her show this level of compassion for a child such as Maggie, much less the attention she showered on Penny. Mary had told Priscilla this morning that her mother had assigned a maid to create a large, fluffy dog bed and had even sketched a picture of what she wanted. The bed was placed on the floor next to Maggie.

"You have another child living here?" The dowager countess beamed. "Of course she and Rose can come. I should like to meet this Maggie."

"And you will, Mama. I shall have us ready to go in fifteen minutes," Priscilla's mother said with a smile.

"Take a few extra minutes if you need it, my dear. I'm going to have a cup of tea to warm my bones," Priscilla's grandmother said cheerfully.

When Priscilla's mother left the room, her grandmother looked up from her cup of tea and gave a questioning look to her son, but neither said a word.

Priscilla and Jane hurried to the sidebar and selected their food. "I'm almost too excited to eat, but if I skip it, I'll pay for it with a growling stomach," said Jane, placing rashers and eggs on her plate.

"Same with me!" Priscilla laughed, choosing the toast and jam, and pouring herself some chocolate.

"Careful with that chocolate, daughter," her father warned good-naturedly.

Her grandmother winked and then sipped her tea.

Did everyone know she had sabotaged her dress on purpose? *No matter,* Priscilla thought cheerily, sipping the chocolate. *This is a chance to find a beautiful dress for the theater.* With Grandmama along, she knew it wouldn't be orange.

TWO CARRIAGES CONTAINING the small entourage turned from St. James onto King Street and stopped in front of the modiste's shop. "It was a good idea to bring the extra carriage," Lady Burleson said to her mother-in-law. "The older girls readily chose to ride together, which let us all spread out."

"Yes," the older woman said with a chuckle. "We will undoubtedly need the extra room for the packages."

Before Lady Burleson's girls entered the modiste's shop, she pulled the two of them aside. "Ladies, while I am focused on Maggie and Rose with this visit, I expect you to carry on with your selections *as if I were with you.*" The countess looked pointedly at Priscilla.

Priscilla looked beyond her mother to see her grandmama wink at her from behind. "We will certainly feel your presence, Mama."

Looking unsure if her edict had been accepted or if she was being ignored, Lady Burleson nodded before turning to the younger girls. She ushered them inside the store to a corner where Madame Soyeuse had a selection of fabrics suitable for their age. "Look at these orange and pink fabrics," Priscilla heard her mother say, and winced.

"Cilla, look at the exquisite fabrics in the window. I think that purple would be perfect on you!" exclaimed Jane, pulling her sister toward the front of the store.

"Girls, you pick out the fabrics you like. I'll take care of the rest," the dowager whispered. "Priscilla, look at the readymade dresses Madame Soyeuse has over in the corner. Some of the fabrics you love are among them, and it might be the best way to find something for tomorrow evening."

"Thank you, Grandmama!" Priscilla said, giving the older woman's hand a slight squeeze.

Priscilla and Jane pored over the fabrics, oohing over each one until each of them had narrowed their choices to three. Jane found an orange-and-pink-patterned fabric that, despite her aversion to the color, Priscilla liked for Jane. Her grandmother found a beautiful deep purple satin with sheer gold overlay in the readymade gowns. "The color is perfect for you!" she gushed.

"I agree. It's perfect for your eyes and hair. And I love these two colors as well," Jane said, pointing out the bolts of teal and royal-blue satin.

"They would be stunning colors for the upcoming Christmastide, my dear," their grandmother enthused.

"I love them," Priscilla agreed, and, seeing her mother across the room with Maggie and Rose, quickly passed them to Madame Soyeuse. The modiste, Priscilla noticed, measured the gown and, once approving, slid the readymade dress and the teal and blue satin fabric beneath bolts already approved by the countess.

Grandmama tittered. "She's learning, I see."

"Madame Soyeuse, I wish to gift everyone in our party a beautiful winter holiday pelisse for Christmastide," she said, withdrawing a bolt of sapphire blue from a stack of wool bolts in the corner. She gestured at the stack. "There will be lots of parties. Choose the color you adore, and we shall have lovely outerwear made."

"How very generous, Mother," said Lady Burleson, feeling the richness of the wool.

"Oh, my lady! Your taste is exceptional! These fabrics just arrived," Madame Soyeuse enthused. "This fabric will make a lovely pelisse!

What about a matching satin lining?"

The countess chose a neutral winter white for herself, claiming it would work with all her gowns, and while Jane agreed, she selected a deep rose color that Madame Soyeuse felt would match the holiday color palette she had just chosen. Pricilla loved the white her mother selected—happily following her lead and commissioning the color for her pelisse. "It will be most versatile." The color was perfect with her hair, and it would match her new green dress. She said nothing but planned to wear the green gown during the upcoming season.

"Winter white is a very modern color choice," Madame Soyeuse said, before pointing out that most ladies of the *ton* selected deeper jewel tones.

The countess selected bright pink for both Maggie and Rose and decided to provide fur muffs for everyone as her gift.

"Ladies, you are most generous," cooed the modiste, smiling broadly. "I have all your measurements and notes on your wishes. We shall have everything ready in a week." Touching a light brown package, she slid it close to the dowager. "I wrapped the dress for Lady Priscilla in this package," she whispered when Lady Burleson became occupied across the room.

The bell on the door tinkled as Lady Albertine and her daughters stepped into the shop.

Both simultaneously taking one of their trademark sighs, Priscilla's mother and grandmother pasted smiles on their faces and turned to the newcomers.

"I see we are all of the same mind today," the dowager countess said, nodding politely to the younger woman. Lady Albertine was well known for her gossiping, and the Burlesons usually avoided her when they were out and about. Unfortunately, the dressmaker's establishment was conducive to such chatter.

Lady Albertine nodded as well but made a beeline for Priscilla's mother. "Oh, Lady Burleson, there is something I must share with you," she prattled. Then, in a self-aggrandizing tone, she added, "But first, allow me to guide my daughters into the dressing rooms for their fittings." She turned to the modiste. "I require your assistance with my daughters."

Grandmama raised a brow as they watched Lady Albertine and her daughters trail behind Madame Soyeuse to the dressing room areas, leaving them alone in the front of the shop.

"I never feel good about a woman who announces she has gossip when she walks into a room," the dowager said. "Perhaps we should conclude our purchases and leave."

The countess nodded and had started for the counter when the odious woman rushed back. "Milly," Lady Albertine said, signaling Lady Burleson to join her in a corner as if they were the best of friends.

Priscilla watched her mother's eyes widen and her expression change to one of shock, and then outrage, as Lady Albertine's hands fluttered, and her lips sputtered. The countess excused herself and returned to complete their purchases, then ushered the two younger children from the store without a word to Jane, Priscilla, or their grandmother.

"What in the world did that busybody say to ignite your mother that way?" Grandmama wondered out loud, before walking up to the woman. "Lady Albertine, I would like to know what you said to my daughter to upset her so."

"I am pleased to share it with you." Donning a look of utter satisfaction, Lady Albertine said, "Your son was seen leaving the private side door of the Lyon's Den yesterday afternoon. One might imagine something untoward with such a visit."

"Like?" Priscilla's grandmother prompted tersely.

"Well, I don't know. One might imagine he has taken either the widow or one of her ladies as a mistress. Of course, I would *never* think such a thing."

"Was seen? By whom?" the dowager demanded impatiently.

"I assure you it is true. I saw it myself."

"And what were you doing there that you saw such a thing—a

man leaving by the side door of the Lyon's Den?" the dowager asked, with raised brows.

Priscilla sucked in her breath as her grandmother's face reddened with rage.

"You can thank God my daughter and granddaughters are ladies. It is unfortunate for you, however, that I am too old to care what Society thinks," she said before slapping Lady Albertine crisply across the face. "Never, ever disparage a member of my family again with your vicious, petty lies." She turned to leave.

"*Well, I never!*" Lady Albertine gasped.

The dowager spun and faced the woman again. "I doubt that very much. And a word of advice, Lady Albertine. You had best tread carefully. I've known you and have endured your destructive antics for years, as has the rest of the *ton*. You are a jealous, loathsome harpy who delights in the pain and misfortune of others. I'm quite certain other *respectable* members of Society would join me in mutual outrage at your latest attempts to cause hurt. I hope you heed my advice. Britain considers defamation a serious crime. If you fail to heed me, I shall make it my business to employ every means at my disposal to see that you do." The dowager turned and gave her granddaughters a firm nod. "Come along, girls. We have far more important things to attend to."

As they exited the shop, Priscilla glanced over her shoulder and couldn't help but grin at the insufferable woman gaping after them, her mouth hanging open in shocked surprise. She was a little in awe of her grandmother and had wanted to break into applause when she stood up to Lady Albertine.

But Priscilla was also worried. Her father would never be unfaithful to her mother, but there could only be one reason why he had been seen at the Lyon's Den. Could he have found out what Priscilla was doing?

"Would you have a few minutes for us to check with the bookstore, Grandmama?" Jane asked as they strolled down the street.

"I should love to pick up a copy of *Frankenstein*. I hear it is enthralling."

"Ah, yes. That oddly titled book has much of the *ton* discussing it—mostly due to its *anonymous* author and their notoriety. But yes, my darling girls, the bookstore sounds delightful." The dowager passed the light brown package she was holding to a waiting footman. "There might be a book or two I desire." With that, the three women entered the nearby bookstore, the door sounding a welcome jingle as they stepped in.

Alex looked up to see Lady Priscilla, her sister, and, if memory served, her grandmother, the Dowager Countess Burleson, enter the store. "My ladies! To what do I owe this great fortune?" He came from behind a bookshelf and stood in front of them.

"We came to pick out a few books. Jane wanted *Frankenstein*," Priscilla said.

"Ah! I *have* heard of that one. You are speaking of a novel that has many in the *ton* speculating about who might have written it." He pointed toward a stack of burgundy leather books on the small table in front of them.

"I see a section of books I might enjoy. Come, Jane," the dowager said, walking across the shop and leaving Alex with Priscilla.

With her family across the room, Alex turned to the bookseller. "My father kept a diary. And I wish to obtain a couple of blank copies for my own needs. Can you point me to the diaries he usually purchased?"

"Certainly, my lord. Your father's death was a tragic loss. He was a loyal and wonderful customer. He trusted me to help him stock his library." The bookseller cleared his throat. "They are located on the end of this aisle." He pointed to the long shelves of books that ran vertically to the store.

"May I see them as well?" Lady Priscilla asked. "I should like to get a copy for my sister and myself."

"I would be happy for your company." Alex turned back to the owner. "Do you recall the color he usually purchased? I must purchase matching books."

"Yes, my lord. I believe it was the navy-blue leather," the bookseller said.

Alex glanced at Priscilla's sister, who, with her grandmother, was engrossed in the burgundy gothic books across the room.

"May I accompany you?" Lady Priscilla asked.

"Yes, of course, my lady." He extended his arm. Lady Priscilla touched it lightly, and a frisson of heat ripped up his arm and to his gut. "I believe these must be them." The top shelf held the books. "What color tome would you like?" he asked, trying to quell the heat in his gut. Attempting to distract himself, he reached for several navy copies and tucked them beneath his arm.

"The teal books are lovely. Might I have two?" she asked. "I plan to gift my sister one."

His hand brushed against her neck as he extracted the books, tucking them into her hands and relishing the warmth that raced through his body.

"Ah, there you are, darling. Jane has made her selection." The dowager noted the diaries in Priscilla's hands. "And it seems you have."

"As have I," Alex said, sliding the three books from under his arm and placing them on the counter.

"My lord, I see you found what you were looking for," the owner said, taking the books and wrapping them. "Shall I add these to your account and have them delivered?"

Alex fought the impulse to purchase all the books, including the ones Lady Jane and her grandmother held. The dowager would believe it to be improper and resist. "You may add them to my account. But I will take them with me. My carriage is waiting."

The shop owner completed the transaction and handed the wrapped parcel to him. "Thank you, Lord Wrotham."

Alex turned to the dowager and her granddaughters. "Ladies, it was wonderful to see you, especially you, Dowager Countess Burleson." He looked at Lady Priscilla, willing the loud staccato of his heart to quiet. "If not for an urgent matter at home, Lady Priscilla, I would gladly escort you ladies home." He gave a roguish smile. "However, I look forward to escorting you to the theater tomorrow night."

Leaving the shop, he glanced back and saw Lady Jane nudge her sister playfully, as Lady Priscilla gazed in his direction. His heart clenched, and a curious feeling rocked him. What was happening to him? He raised his hand to wave, but then clenched it closed, feeling hesitant.

Alex felt closer than ever to achieving his pursuit, but his goals were blurring suddenly. Her father had asked him to watch her, but when had she become important to him? *One thing at a time,* he reminded himself. *First, I must find that diary. Father's good name and my mother's heart are at stake.* Tonight, he planned to tear the study apart; he would find the missing diary. And he would find out more about his supposed *cousin*, Lord Franklin Anders.

Amid his angst over the diary, his mind pivoted to his brief interlude with Lady Priscilla and her gorgeous, sparkling lavender eyes and full lips. Each time he saw her, he found himself under her spell—imagining beautiful auburn locks sprawled across his pillow, with him paused just above her rose-colored lips. A torment for his body, but a salve to his heart. She was the dream he never imagined could be his reality.

Tomorrow—you will see her tomorrow, his heart screamed.

Chapter Thirteen

"To what do I owe the pleasure of your visit, Lady Burleson?" Mrs. Dove-Lyon asked. The widow waved her hand, simultaneously dismissing her footman and indicating the woman should sit. She indicated a decanter to her left. "May I offer you some refreshment?"

"No thank you." Lady Burleson shot her a look of disgust as she smoothed out her skirt.

"Well then, you won't mind my having a small glass," Bessie said, pouring herself a small glass and taking a sip.

While the woman stared malevolently in her direction, Bessie noticed her bottom lip tremble slightly. "Lady Burleson, what has you so upset?" She took another sip.

The woman flashed her a look of disdain. "You can tell me what my husband was doing here. I have been told you—or one of the women in your employ—have become his mistress."

Bessie spluttered after her coughing fit stopped. "Excuse me?" The widow dabbed at her lips from beneath her black veil. She decided against inviting her guest to use her given name. They may have been casual acquaintances in the past, because of their husbands' close association, but in truth, she barely tolerated Burleson's wife, detesting the woman's condescending air of superiority.

Bessie regarded the woman, struggling over what she should say. A strange series of events had placed her in this awkward position, when her only transgression had been helping an erstwhile friend's rebel daughter stay safe. "May I ask who told you your husband was here?" Bessie asked coolly.

"You may. Lady Albertine delighted in telling me that she saw him leaving in the middle of the day. So, why was he here?"

Bessie set her drink on the desk, no longer feeling thirsty. What she wanted to do was wring a certain woman's neck—well, maybe two women's necks, she thought, as she considered the one in front of her. She took a deep breath.

"Settle yourself, *Mildred*." Her tone was reproachful. "I am not interested in an affair with your husband, and he is not having an affair with any of my employees," Bessie said. "I suggest you consider your source. Has it occurred to you that outside of those who own businesses here, there are only a handful of reasons people visit this end of Cleveland Avenue?" She paused for effect. "However, I generally do not divulge the business of my… uh… clientele. But I can say that, to my knowledge, Mrs. Albertine owns no property in this area."

The woman paled, but Bessie disregarded it. Lady Albertine's odd proclivities would no longer be accommodated; she would let the woman know her visits to the Lyon's Den were at an end. "Now, as to your husband—who was the best friend of my own dear Sandstrom—you should be ashamed. To my knowledge, he has no mistress, but if he did, who could blame him?" Incensed at being drawn into this ludicrous fight between these two women, Bessie leaned forward. "The man is a saint, having been married to you all these years." She drew a fortifying breath. "He was here because of your daughter."

"M-my daughter?" Lady Burleson pulled back in shock. "What has my daughter to do with his visits here?"

Bessie bristled but maintained a cool façade. "Do you really want to know? I warn you, it may not be what you expect to hear."

Lady Burleson visibly gulped. "I do. And I demand you tell me immediately," she huffed.

Bessie gave a wry half-smile. "Of course. And we do want to meet your every demand," she intoned. "Your daughter dresses as a man named Mr. Paul Smith and comes here regularly to gamble. She has it in her head that she needs financial independence *from you*. According to what I know, you parade her and her sister, Lady Jane, in front of the *ton*, when you must be aware—unless you are deaf—of their... *limited* musical ability. You do it because it allows you to flex your power and influence within Society, while your daughters suffer and are often made the butt of jokes. And your daughter, Priscilla, has a stutter—which worsens in those humiliating situations.

"Furthermore—at eight and ten years of age, you demand she wears fabrics only you approve, and as a result, she dresses like a puffed-up parrot. You choose outlandish colors that make her red hair look like the top of a torch. Lady Priscilla is a beautiful woman in her own right, but you refuse her any latitude to display her gifts. Instead, you demand she dress like a peacock. So, she dresses like a man and plays cards, gambling to win funds and gain her independence from an impossible situation."

Bessie shut her eyes and took a deep breath. When she opened them, she was shocked to see tears streaming down Lady Burleson's face.

"I probably went too far," Bessie said, immediately regretting her temper. She reached into her pocket and withdrew a white lace handkerchief. Stepping from behind her desk, she handed it to Lady Burleson and took the seat next to her.

"No." Mildred sniffed. "What you say is true, although I never saw it that way. I swear!"

"What do you say we both have a well-deserved glass of sherry?" Oddly, Bessie believed her. Her husband was a fair man—a good man. She trusted there was more to this lady than met the eye.

"Please call me Milly," Lady Burleson said, sniffling into the lacy cloth and referencing Bessie's not-so-subtle slight. "Mildred was my mother's name, and I have hated it from birth."

Bessie slapped her leg lightly and laughed. "How about some refreshments?" Without waiting for an answer, she rang for assistance.

A tall man stepped inside.

"Devon, could you get us two clean glasses and a decanter of sherry? And have the cook send up some cheese, fruit, and those delectable cucumber sandwiches she makes. We require a bit of refreshment."

"Yes, Mrs. Dove-Lyon." The man stooped, opened the ornate liquor cabinet on the wall behind them, and withdrew the decanter of sherry. Stepping over to the two women, he filled two glasses with a liberal amount.

When he had gone, Bessie turned to Milly. "I'm afraid I was extremely harsh. But when you mentioned that Albertine woman's name, I just lost it."

"She does that to me as well," Milly confessed, smiling weakly. "She crashed a perfectly lovely outing with my girls and my mother-in-law at the modiste's to tell me of my husband's alleged infidelity. I'm afraid rational thought abandoned me, and I hurried over here."

"Yes… what do you say we start over? We are old friends, after all," Bessie said, squeezing Milly's hand.

Milly sniffed. "Yes, I suppose we are… or should be. I apologize for my ghastly behavior."

"And I apologize for—"

"No, don't." She held up a gloved hand. "You have nothing to apologize for. Not even my husband would have spoken to me thus. I needed to hear *all of that*—they were things I should have known. But I was too… *puffed up*… to recognize what I was doing to my darling daughters."

Hearing the use of her own words, Bessie giggled, causing them both to laugh.

Devon knocked and entered with tea and a tray of refreshments.

"Set it there, Devon. We can serve ourselves."

"Very good, Mrs. Dove-Lyon," he said, and left.

"Let's save the tea for after our sherry," the widow suggested.

Milly nodded with a mouthful of sandwiches. "Please tell me about my daughter. I had no idea she was slipping away from the house." She visibly shook.

"Your daughter threatened to go elsewhere if I wouldn't permit her to gamble here. I couldn't allow that because I wouldn't be able to secure the safety of my husband's dearest friend's daughter. So, I relented, with certain provisions," Bessie explained. "Mr. Smith must arrive in a hackney and exit from the door of the hackney into the side of the building. Titus watches over her while she is here, and he sees her into a trusted hackney when she leaves. We don't let her stay overlong." She sipped her sherry for a moment. "She is very talented with cards."

"How did my husband find out she was coming here?"

"Lord Wrotham told him. The earl figured out who he—that is, Mr. Paul Smith—was shortly after your ball. Something about a mole on her face," the widow said. "Anyway, concerned, he went to your husband."

"Yes. It is a beautiful mark," the countess said, swiping at a rogue tear.

"If you will permit me to say, I have a feeling about these two. Lord Wrotham's concern warrants some consideration. He wouldn't have agreed to court over your daughter if he had no interest. Of course, it is merely a fake courtship—at least on his part—to my understanding."

Milly tapped her glass with her forefinger. "I'm not sure. He danced two waltzes with her at my ball."

Bessie raised her brows and looked knowingly at Milly. "Would you find the man objectionable for your daughter?"

Milly looked at the widow in astonishment. "No. I should say not. I would be the envy of the *ton*…" She let the sentence drop and gave a sheepish smile. "No, I think he may be perfect for her, and my daughter would probably have little objection as well. He has asked her to the theater with his family."

The widow clapped her hands in glee. "This arrangement has potential!"

Bessie and Milly spent another hour sharing stories, with Bessie discovering they had more in common than she would have imagined.

"I must take my leave, but I appreciate the many kindnesses. And your frankness," Milly said, noticing she was still holding the white lacy linen. "Allow me to clean your handkerchief and return it. There are many things I must fix—starting with my daughters' perception of me. It was hard to hear." She stood.

"Kindly consider me your friend and check in with me at any time." Bessie stood and gave her new friend a hug. "You have a solid backbone, my dear, and I admire you. I feel that is a rarity among the *ton*. As a mother, you are charged with seeing your daughters settled. I shall consider us cohorts in this venture."

"I appreciate your kindness. Thank you for everything, Bessie."

When the door opened, Titan stood ready.

"Titan, please show Lady Burleson to her carriage," the widow said.

"Your carriage awaits at the side door, my lady."

Milly nodded. "Thank you, Titan."

ALEX SYSTEMATICALLY REMOVED everything from the drawers of his desk and replaced them. He felt beneath the desk, looking for a secret panel—any place that could hide a diary. Nothing. Methodically, he began at one end of the room, pulling books from the shelves and stacking them back.

"What in the world are you doing?" his mother said, appearing behind him.

"Mother, I wasn't expecting you."

"Obviously not. Why are you ripping your study apart?"

He laid the armload of books on the floor and stood to face his mother. "You mentioned a diary Father kept. And you said you wished to read it."

"So, because I am missing a book, you decided to destroy your study?" She narrowed her eyes. "Pray tell, son. What is going on with you?"

He walked to one of the leather seats in front of his desk. "Come sit down, Mother. I suppose it is time I told you."

"Told me *what?*"

"Father left us in debt." Alex couldn't bear to hurt his mother, but there seemed little way around it.

"How is that possible? You have said nothing."

"No, and I believe we are finally free of that yoke. But Father was taken in by some unscrupulous people."

"You must mean that horrid Lord Anders. The man spent months trying to convince your father to support him in some sort of venture in America."

Alex realized his mouth was hanging open and closed it. "Why is this the first I am hearing of it?"

"Frankly, because I had forgotten in all the pain surrounding your father's passing last year." She turned to the side and wiped a tear from her face. "The man practically camped at our front door until, I suppose, your father agreed to the business arrangement. It had something to do with steam engines in America."

"But why would he agree to invest in a country where he had no one to protect his interests?"

"I'm not sure. But your father kept all that sort of stuff in the diaries."

"How long did Father keep diaries?"

"As long as I knew him. And the last diary—maybe two—is missing. They would have the details of the last couple of years of his life."

"That's what I deduced, and why I've been tearing the room apart." If Anders had owed his father money, why had there been nothing in the ledgers? He decided not to mention Mrs. Marble at this time. Perhaps it would be necessary later. But the information on Anders produced more questions. "Mother, I've heard something about Anders being a distant cousin. Can it be true?"

She shrugged. "I suppose it could be. Your father never considered him family, so I'm not aware of them being related. However, we have a family Bible that could help." She walked to a bookcase that Alex had not reached yet, and as she stepped near it, the floor creaked. Ignoring that, she removed the heavy book from its spot. "Alex, come look at this. It's a button of some sort. You can barely see it." She pressed it, and a nearby floorboard sounded like it popped up.

Moving away, she rolled back the corner of the dark green Aubusson carpet to reveal several floorboards joined together that had popped up slightly. "I've never seen this."

"Neither have I," Alex admitted, studying the open cavity vacated by the floorboards. A sheen of dust covered two small stacks of ledgers and books. Two leather-bound books sat next to them. Withdrawing his handkerchief, he wiped the surface of the books. They matched the ones he had purchased from the bookstore. "I think we've located the diaries, Mother. If not for your help, I don't think we would have found them."

The countess smiled and swiped at tears. Stooping, she picked up one of the stacked books. "These must be diaries as well." Opening one, she pointed to the date. "These were written before we married."

"The family connection to Lord Anders could be in one of those." Alex thumbed through the book he held. "It appears these entries begin a little over a year before Father's death. Would you mind if I read through this one, Mother? I promise to give it to you, but I feel there is so much to glean, and I'd like time to read through it."

"I cannot believe he was able to write. It makes me think we might have missed something." Her voice sounded thick with emotion. She glanced at the other one. "This is from two years before his death. Would you mind terribly if I took this one? If I see anything that looks like something you could use, I will bring it to your attention."

"I think that is a good use of our time. Two sets of eyes on these would be better." Alex was already trying to decide what to do with entries concerning Mrs. Delores Marble. He couldn't allow his mother to be hurt.

"I have the others that I've finished. Should we place them here? Or would you have a better suggestion?"

"Perhaps we should decide what Father would want to do with them," Alex replied.

"Good idea, son. He would want them accessible for all four of us—you, me, Thomas, and Louisa. I suspect they contain valuable information about the estate, its history, and its management. I confess to skipping through some of that."

Impulsively, he hugged her close and kissed her on the cheek.

"I love you, Alex."

"I love you too, Mother. I don't tell you enough."

"Well..." she said, sounding a little flummoxed, "if you agree, I will retire to my chamber. His diaries have been my way to reconnect with George."

He nodded and watched his mother pick up a few of the books and leave the room. Alex planned to read as much as he could tonight, praying his mother wasn't going to be hurt through all of this—although he wasn't sure that was possible.

Chapter Fourteen

The next day

"Darling, when you get dressed, please join us in the breakfast room."

Still groggy, Priscilla sat up in the bed feeling thoroughly confused. "Mama, am I late for breakfast?"

Uncharacteristically, her mother walked over and bussed Priscilla's cheek. "Not at all. I have something important to discuss."

A cold frisson of dread passed through her. "We aren't having… another g-gathering, are we?"

Her mother gave a tremulous smile. "Not at all. I just have something to say, my darling." She stopped at the door and turned back. "I love you, Priscilla. I don't say it enough."

Truthfully, Priscilla couldn't recall the last time her mother had told her she loved her. Of course, she knew she did. It just wasn't said.

The door closed behind her mother.

A moment later, Jane opened it and jumped up on Priscilla's bed. "Cilla, did Mama tell you to come downstairs? Grandmama just arrived. What's going on?"

"I've no idea. At first, I feared another musicale or party. But when I asked, she said no."

"She's been acting strange. Yesterday when she came home, she made a beeline for Papa's study. They've been acting differently all morning."

Priscilla eyed her sister. "Did you listen?"

"Of course not!" Jane tried to maintain a straight face, but it crumpled into laughter and the two girls fell on their backs on the bed, laughing. "It's the only way we know what's going on, you know."

"And I'm most appreciative of the sacrifice you make to spy," Priscilla said, giggling and feeling more relaxed than she had in a while. If Mama wasn't announcing a musicale, she could deal with it.

The door opened, and Mary walked in with a tray of biscuits and two cups of chocolate. "Ladies, your mama wishes to see you both downstairs. I brought you chocolate. But we must hurry."

Twenty minutes later, Priscilla and Jane scurried downstairs. As they approached the breakfast room, Priscilla could hear her grandmother speaking to her father.

"I cannot recall the last time I was summoned, my dear. Does this have something to do with that horrid woman, Lady Albertine?"

"I cannot say."

"Can't or won't?" her grandmother said. "Where is Milly, anyway?"

"She will be here, Mother," Lord Burleson said.

Priscilla and Jane walked in and took their seats. Seeing her father and Grandmama had already served themselves, she elbowed her sister and pointed to the sideboard, where they filled their plates.

"Darling, tonight is the night you attend the theater with Lord Wrotham, correct?"

Priscilla's face heated. "It is." Grandmama winked in her direction. Madame Soyeuse had wrapped a beautiful dress for her to wear, which needed no alterations. Her only problem was getting past Mama. She would think of something, she decided.

"Good, I'm glad everyone is here," her mother said, entering the room and closing the door behind her. She took her seat next to her husband. He reached for her hand, clasping it tightly, and gave her a reassuring look.

"Yesterday became a rather difficult day for me. Not only did she ruin our wonderful outing, but Lady Albertine's malicious gossip sent me on the road of reflection—something I'm afraid was too long in coming. Initially, I was furious and acted badly. But soon, I was reminded by a friend of my faults. And they are considerable." She turned to her two eldest daughters. "First and foremost, I apologize to both of you for feeding my ego by using you two to perform musicales. I knew you weren't comfortable, yet I persisted, feeling they would gain you notoriety in the *ton*. That happened, but it wasn't what I had intended." Her gaze locked with Priscilla. "I'm especially sorry about what I've done to you, Priscilla. Jane and I share similar coloring and can wear the same fabric colors, but you take after your beautiful grandmother. And stubbornly, I denied you colors that complemented your coloring, thinking what worked for me would work for you." Tears streamed down her face. "I am so sorry."

"Mama, it is not nec—" Priscilla started.

"No, please, let me finish," her mother said, holding up a hand. "My apology is heartfelt and needed."

Grandmama cleared her throat. "Let us move past this," she said, surprising everyone. "You have apologized, Milly."

"You left before the main event, Mama. Grandmama took Lady Albertine down a few pegs," Jane said excitedly.

Lady Burleson looked at her mother-in-law. "Y-you did that for me?"

"Pish! You are my son's wife—and a member of my family. Family looks out for family, no matter what disagreements in the past."

"Thank you," Lady Burleson replied. She looked at Priscilla. "Do you have any other 'secret' gowns, my dear?"

Priscilla felt her mouth go dry as she looked from her mother to her grandmother, who gave a subtle nod. "I do. It was a dress I found readymade."

"And Grandmama approved?"

Numbly, Priscilla nodded.

Lady Burleson said, "Then I'm certain it will be perfect for the theater. We will replace those orange, green, and pink dresses. And for you as well, Jane. You can select colors that bring you happiness, not disquiet."

"I suggest we finish this lovely breakfast, ladies," said Lord Burleson, then he turned to his wife and kissed her on the cheek.

The dowager coughed, drawing their attention. "I consented to accompany my dear friend, Lady Florence Mathers, and her family to the theater—so you may see me during intermission, granddaughter. I assure you it was before Lord Wrotham asked you, although I think Lord Mathers has a rather prominent box as well."

"Oh?" her son asked.

"It will be comforting to know you are there, Grandmama," Priscilla said.

"Just the same, I don't want you to feel you are being spied upon." Grandmama smiled, and everyone laughed in relief.

Priscilla had the distinct feeling her grandmother's opera glasses would be trained on her, rather than on the play.

A strange, gurgling, songlike duet suddenly erupted from the kitchen. Everyone looked at one another.

"Does your cook yodel?" Grandmother asked.

A footman stepped inside the breakfast room to refresh the sideboard. "Anson, what was that?" Lord Burleson asked.

Anson's lips twitched. "I'm not quite sure, my lord. It is the dog and the little girl, Maggie. I think they are singing together. I've never seen anything like it."

"Really?" Lady Burleson asked in astonishment. "I've never heard such a thing. Please ask them to join us."

"Yes, my lady."

"Are you sure, Milly? You have rules against animals in here," her husband said.

"Pish! Penny is no regular animal," she returned, leaving everyone in the room momentarily gaping in astonishment.

Maggie and her dog appeared in the doorway.

"Don't just stand there, my dear. Join us and bring your... Penny," Grandmama encouraged the girl.

Maggie glanced nervously around the room, while Penny wagged her tail and began to sniff beneath the table. Priscilla looked warily at her mother.

"Maggie, did we hear you and your dog singing... together?" Mama asked in astonishment.

"Yes, my lady. 'Tis something we did to take our minds off the cold," the little girl replied nervously. "We do everything together."

"We are most curious. Would you be able to sing for us?" Grandmama asked gently.

Maggie nodded and softly cradled the dog's face, gaining her attention. "Penny. One... two..."

"O wooo woowoo, wooo woowoo, woo..." the dog began, singing a few notes and then giving her best smile.

"My pretty little baby, please don't cry..." Maggie chimed in softly, tapping her foot as their voices blended.

When she had finished, Penny gave everyone her best smile. Maggie patted her on the head and kissed her.

"I believe I recognized that," Grandmama said, clasping her hands together in astonishment. She looked at Maggie. "You did a lovely job, Maggie. It sounded very much like the lullaby my mother sang to me when I was a child."

Maggie smiled. "M'mum sang it to me before I went to sleep.

When she died, I sang it to myself. One day, Penny started singing with me." She hugged her dog's neck.

The room was silent, and Priscilla saw her mother and grandmother wipe tears away.

Papa grabbed a rasher from his plate and handed it to the dog. "Darling wife, I believe with a little work, you may be able to replicate those musicales after all!"

"She sings in tune," his wife mused out loud. "Maggie, do you think you and your dog might learn a short Christmastide song?"

"We could try, m'lady," Maggie said thoughtfully.

"Please, my dear. Join us." Lady Burleson patted the seat next to her.

"Perhaps a lovely orange wrap for the dog would be nice," Grandmama added, causing everyone to laugh.

Lord Burleson said, hooting, "Now, I have heard everything."

Priscilla couldn't recall a time when she and her sister had laughed as much with their family over a meal. She hated seeing breakfast end.

Later that night

"CILLA, HIS CARRIAGE just pulled up! Are you sure you don't need me with you?" Jane asked, taunting her sister.

"I will be well chaperoned with his mother and sister. Father had already approved me to go with just his family, sis, or I would take you. I'm sorry." Priscilla wished she had pushed to take her sister. Her stomach was a mass of nerves.

She took a lingering look at herself in her looking glass. She barely recognized the woman wearing the deep purple gown with a sheer gold overlay. Her mother had loaned her the amethyst earrings her father had given her for their wedding.

"Stunning, my dear," her mother said. She held out a beautiful ecru white wool pelisse with gold-threaded embroidery. "Please wear this."

"I would love to, Mama," Priscilla said, taking the pelisse and holding it to her face. "It's incredibly soft."

"It has always been my favorite. Your grandmama had it made for me years ago. It'll make her smile to see you wearing it."

Jane and their mother followed Priscilla to the front parlor, where Lord Alex Wrotham waited.

Alex turned when she entered the room, his vanilla and patchouli scent wafted toward her, and she drank in the vision of him. He was dressed in a black jacket and britches with a silver brocade waistcoat. Wavy chestnut-brown hair barely cleared the collar of his coat, setting off a beautifully knotted cravat, anchored by a diamond stickpin.

"You look lovely, Lady Priscilla," he said, sketching a bow. "These are for you." Lord Wrotham withdrew a bouquet of white roses bound in a green ribbon from behind him. As he handed them to her, heat came through his gloved hand, and butterflies swarmed her stomach.

"Thank you, Lord Wrotham. They are my favorite." Priscilla had never received flowers and fought the impulse to bury her face in their essence. She loved roses, especially white ones.

"A favor," he said, smiling down into her eyes. "For tonight, may we dispense with lord and lady? Let us be Alex and Priscilla."

She held his gaze and smiled, nodding. "I would like that, Alex."

Hearing steps in the hall, he took a step back, and she leaned into the roses, inhaling their fragrance and promising herself to remember this moment forever.

"Arlington, please place these lovely flowers in a vase and put them in Lady Priscilla's room," her mother said, entering the room on the arm of her husband.

Priscilla handed the flowers to the butler, savoring the mixture of roses and vanilla in the air.

"Wrotham, it is good to see you." Lord Burleson kissed his daughter on the cheek. "Take special care of my daughter, Wrotham."

"It shall be my pleasure," Alex said, his words sending a slight quiver down Priscilla's spine. Something about their exchange made her feel like she had missed something.

"I suppose we should get going," he said, accepting her pelisse from the butler and placing it around her shoulders.

"Have a lovely time, darling," her mother said, taking Priscilla's gloved hands in hers and squeezing them.

Priscilla leaned in and kissed her mother. "I will, Mama. I cannot wait to see *Romeo and Juliet*," she whispered.

WROTHAM'S FAMILY SETTLED in their box in the upper levels of Drury Lane. Priscilla took her seat in the front of the box, noticing that Alex sat directly behind her, with his brother to his right. Lady Louisa took the seat to her right, and Lady Wrotham the one to her left.

Priscilla scanned the room, anxious to see if her grandmother had already been seated. She spotted a well-dressed woman with graying red hair directly across from her with her opera glasses trained on their box. The woman withdrew her opera glasses and nodded in her direction. *Grandmama.*

The lights were lowered, and the noise died as the play began. Priscilla found herself enthralled in the story. She had always loved the story of unrequited love, but this was the first time she had seen it in a theater—something she would never forget. She leaned forward in her seat and followed every scene, not taking her eyes off the stage until the curtain went down for intermission.

"Would you like to stretch your legs and get something to drink?" Alex asked, lightly touching her shoulder, and sending a delightful sensation across her shoulders.

She glanced at the countess, who nodded. "I would love to," Priscilla replied, looking into his vivid gray eyes. Standing, she picked up her pelisse and followed his lead from the box.

Theater hallways weren't known for their warmth, so he held the coat while she slipped into her pelisse as they left the box. Taking the stairs, he reached down and gently squeezed her hand.

"Would you enjoy a glass of wine?" he asked, checking the available refreshments.

"I would," she said, then accepted the proffered glass and took a sip. With the crowded ante area, she was glad he had selected white wine, conscious of her mother's beautiful pelisse.

He led her to a corner of the room that had attracted fewer people. He placed his cane down and removed his gloves. "I cannot drink wine wearing gloves. I'm always afraid the glass will slip from my hand."

She giggled, realizing she had also removed hers and stuffed them in her reticule. "I suppose it's a habit of mine, as well." She couldn't help but notice they seemed so comfortable together.

"Do you come to the theater often?" he asked.

"Not as much as I would like." Priscilla scanned the room, loving the glamour of the theater. "I enjoy seeing my favorite stories acted." The acting wasn't always consistent, and sometimes she thought there was as much improvising as learned lines. But tonight, she couldn't take her eyes off the actors. One actress in particular seemed to speak straight to their box tonight, as if they were the only people in attendance. The attention mesmerized her.

"Shall we return to the box?" he asked.

"Yes, I don't want to miss anything. And your mother may wish to stretch her legs."

"They already are." He directed her attention across the room, where his mother stood talking to her grandmother.

Seeing Priscilla, Grandmama excused herself and approached them. "You are wearing that lovely pelisse, my darling. The soft winter white suits you, as it did your dear mama."

"Thank you, Grandmama. It's much warmer than the one I have been wearing."

Her grandmother's keen attention had turned to Alex, and Priscilla felt herself take a step back so they wouldn't appear so close.

"Lord Wrotham, it is wonderful to see your family. I was surprised to find your mother remained in town for Christmas—but happy to learn of it. She looks lovely, as usual. I don't think the woman ever ages." She gave a light laugh.

"Thank you, my lady. I'm certain the feeling is mutual." He looked from Priscilla to the dowager. "I had never given thought to where you got that lovely mane of red hair, Lady Priscilla. And if you will forgive my cheekiness, Lady Burleson, I see where she got her lavender eyes as well."

Grandmama blushed. "Well, if you are gushing compliments, young man, I am happy to allow you a bit of cheekiness." Alex's lips lifted in a wry smile. "I consider it part of my duty to speak the truth."

The older woman glanced in the direction of her friend, who was still speaking with Alex's mother. "I should return to dear Florence. It should be time to get back to our seats, and it takes more time to climb those stairs than it did in my younger days."

A bell sounded, indicating that intermission was ending. "We should return as well," Alex said.

Priscilla accepted his extended arm, and they entered the stairwell they had used to come down. It was darker than the central staircase, and much less crowded, something Priscilla greatly appreciated. They appeared to be alone in the stairwell, which was lit only by an occasional sconce.

As they rounded a darkened turn, he turned to her. "May I kiss you, Priscilla?" he said thickly, his breath already close enough to tickle her neck. Edging closer, he gazed down at her. "I have wanted to kiss you since your family's ball."

Her lips formed an O, and she gave a slight nod. Stepping closer, he closed the gap between them, gently pushing her heatedly against the wall. Running his hand down the side of her face, he traced her chin and then her lips. She wanted to lick them but didn't want to lose this moment. It was as if she had stepped into her recurring dreams of Alex, where he would kiss her in a dark corner.

He leaned into her and slanted his mouth, and both breathed heavily as their bodies pressed together. As he covered her lips and explored her opened mouth, she could taste the wine on his breath and feel the racing of their combined heartbeats. Her senses filled with the smell of his patchouli and vanilla scent, wine, and soap. One hand stretched around his neck, while her right hand slid onto his chest. It felt magical. After a long moment, he pulled back, but touched a finger across her lips, signaling she should stay quiet.

For a moment, neither said a thing. It was the sound of footsteps and voices moving toward them that finally registered with her. Luckily, he had heard it before she had.

When they arrived on the floor where his family box was located, the hall was empty, and she focused on calming her breathing.

"That was nice," he whispered. "Exactly like I had imagined. You are very beautiful."

"Thank you, Alex." Her gaze never left his eyes.

"We had best return before we are missed," he said.

She wanted to stay where they were, with his finger trailing the edges of her face, and his lips caressing hers. It was the stuff of dreams… except this kiss had been real.

When they entered the box, she saw that his family had just arrived. His mother arched a brow in her son's direction, but he merely smiled at her. Priscilla's heart pounded in her ears, and she feared Louisa could hear it. Willing her breathing to slow, she noticed the box where Grandmama sat with opera glasses trained in her direction.

The curtain opened for the next act. Priscilla stared at the stage, willing herself to hear Romeo's soliloquy, but all she heard was Alex asking to kiss her and his heartbeat mingling with hers. When she closed her eyes to clear her thoughts, she saw his lips lowering to hers. Over and over.

Chapter Fifteen

The next day

"Where have you been, dear sister?" Lord Anders lay propped against her pillows, with his feet crossed at the ankles on the sheets she had just laid out for that evening.

Goodness, the sight of him nauseated her. *"Where* do you think?" she snapped. "I've been *working*—something you should acquaint yourself with. Then stealing wouldn't be such an urgency for you." She walked past her bed and heaved his feet off her clean linens. "Move off my bed, Franklin."

Anders wobbled slightly until he regained his place against her pillows. "Damn you, Dee."

"My name is *Delores*. You do not have leave to call me Dee, *Frankie.*"

"Careful," he said, kicking off his boots. "Ah. That's more comfortable." He wiggled his toes. "Sorry for the smell. My valet quit, and they've not had a cleaning in a while."

"That smells worse than the leavings in the gutter," she said. Once upon a time, she had felt grateful to find a half-brother, but no longer.

This man would be her undoing. "You need to leave, especially since you don't want our relationship known to the *ton*. Your father went to great lengths to avoid that, and with all that's riding on this, I think he was right," she sniped. "My every movement is being watched. Your presence in my room was, no doubt, noted."

"Relax. You worry too much. If anyone asks, I'll tell them you weren't worth my coin for the night."

"Does that make you feel smarter... more virile?" she taunted him. "No one with a brain would believe you are anything but a puny English lord. It is not my fault your father favored my mother over yours."

He narrowed his eyes. "I hate my mother, so disparaging her means nothing. The stupid men you told me to use now sit in Newgate after being outmaneuvered by Wrotham and Montgomery. They are the ones that showed your involvement, my dear." His voice lowered. "Your mistake was underestimating me—something you continue to do."

Something in his voice alarmed her. It made no sense that anyone questioned her alleged affair with the older Lord Wrotham. She had done this repeatedly and never had a problem. Everything had gone according to plan. The former Lord Wrotham had been old and slowly become confused... and died. What could have gone wrong?

He had given her money—well, it wasn't given, *exactly*. She stole it from under his nose. And when Wrotham had mentioned a newly gained townhouse, she wanted that, too. This townhouse was hers. *Hers*. She had earned it.

When the play had finally ended, Delores Marble had dabbed beads of sweat from her forehead with a small towel and made her way to her room. It was the second week of production, and her role as Lady Montague had been more arduous than usual, especially since rehearsal time had been so limited because of the nearly back-to-back productions. As a result, she'd made up most of her lines—some of which she thought sounded better than Shakespeare's.

She snorted. No need to worry about the one or two people that may have watched the play instead of each other. No one came to Drury Lane to watch the plays, she reasoned.

A shorter rehearsal schedule and unplanned complications in her personal life had upset her life's normal rhythm. Worse, her half-brother's continual harassment and demands for her help with his business and gaming losses threatened her security. Now, the son of the man who used to own her townhouse had her every move watched and appeared immune to her charms.

"Why are you here?" she demanded.

"Give me something I can use… and not two brainless men."

"Get off my bed and out of my room. One of those brainless men was your footman. You chose him yourself. This is the last thing I'm telling you. I saw Lord Wortham's family box last night. There was a young woman there with red hair. I am unfamiliar with her, but maybe you know her."

"Red hair? Anything else?"

"Seriously? I was on the stage. You figure this out, Franklin."

He dragged himself off her bed and picked up his shoes.

"Put them on before you walk out that door," she ground out.

Anders pulled on his boots and walked to her door. "I will explore the opportunity the red-haired woman gives me."

"Good," she said, shutting the door behind him.

ANDERS LEFT HIS half-sister's room, furious over her insults and unobserved by anyone. "How dare you insult me?" he muttered. His mind reeled through every redheaded woman he could think of, but none were of the type Lord Wrotham would find suitable. "I will find this woman and decide her value. But you, dear sister... you are *expendable*."

"Did you enjoy the play?" Grandmama asked, poking her head in Priscilla's room.

"Come in, Grandmama. This is a pleasant surprise." Priscilla's face broke into a smile. "And yes, I had a wonderful time."

"Does Lord Wrotham plan to see you again?"

Priscilla's face heated. Her grandmother could get right to the point. "I'm not sure. I mean, I like him very much and would enjoy seeing him again. But we barely spoke."

"Pish! Conversation is overrated sometimes. Quiet time together can be just as effective, if not more." Grandmama arched a brow to emphasize her point. "Besides, I noticed how long it took the two of you to return to that box."

"You were *watching?*" Priscilla asked, feigning astonishment. Heat flooded her neck and face.

"Oh, pish!" the older woman scoffed, and tugged her shawl closer. "But of course! What good are opera glasses if not for spying on one's granddaughter and the most eligible bachelor in the theater?"

"The pelisse Mama loaned me kept me very warm. It was astounding how frigid the larger open areas were. And I got several compliments on it. She said you gave it to her years ago."

"I did. And I was quite pleased to see you wear it. The pelisses I am having made this year will follow that pattern. Perhaps one day you will loan it to your daughter," she said with a chuckle, then took a chair close to Priscilla's fireplace. "It's quite toasty in here," she mused.

"It is! Mary stoked the logs when she woke me." A giggle escaped. "I should get my lazy self out of bed, but I am enjoying my new book so much, I didn't wish to budge."

"I had forgotten how comfortable your room is. It suits you, my dear."

Priscilla laid down her book and looked at her grandmother, at the graying hair. But there was more. She looked troubled. "Is something a problem, Grandmama?"

"Perhaps that is something you can answer for me," her grandmother replied, folding her hands in her lap. "I feel there is something amiss, but I cannot quite put my finger on it."

Priscilla's heart gave a nervous jolt. She hated to disappoint her grandmother. The dear woman would think nothing of stepping in front of a runaway carriage to save any member of her family.

"Your mother left Madame Soyeuse's in a hurry, and according to Anson, your footman, he dropped Maggie and Rose here, leaving them with the governess, and had him drive her to Cleveland Row." She paused, probably for effect.

Priscilla gulped. *Grandmama knows… and possibly Mama knows.*

"That's not a location where *proper* ladies go. I know she did it because of Lady Albertine, who said she had seen your father there. We won't discuss Lady Albertine. Goodness knows, there are stories out there that allude to her strange… proclivities."

I always knew there was something not right about that woman, Priscilla thought, summoning up her gumption. "Grandmama, what has this to do with me?"

The older woman regarded her granddaughter closely and tapped the seat of the chair next to her with her hand.

Priscilla sat up and swung her legs over the side of her bed, pushing her feet into her slippers and her wrapper about her shoulders. She plopped into the chair next to her grandmother and curled her feet beneath her, under her robe.

The dowager held the gaze of her granddaughter and squeezed her hand, reminding Priscilla of how formidable her grandmother could be. "That is what I'd like you to tell me."

A lump rose in Priscilla's throat. She couldn't recall ever lying to her grandmother, and now this scheme of hers had her lying to… *everyone*.

"You either are waiting for me to go first, or I am, hopefully, mistaken," Grandmama ruminated.

Priscilla stayed quiet, slowly sliding the trembling hand beneath her skirt.

"I cannot feel right asking your father, but if he was at the Lyon's Den, it would not have been for *activities*." The dowager held Priscilla's gaze. "He would have been there to see the widow, who was the wife of his dearest friend… but not as a mistress. The woman may own a gambling den, but she would resort to such a thing." She drew a breath. "Am I getting warm?" she prodded, none too subtly.

Priscilla closed her eyes, summoning her courage. Grandmama knew, so there was no use in making excuses. "What do you suspect me of doing?" Her eyes filled with unshed tears.

"Darling girl, I don't *suspect* you of anything. I merely want you to admit what you are doing, so we can face this together and find a more reasonable solution. I know my son and your mother. And unless my son has suddenly gained habits that go against his character…"

"He hasn't, Grandmama. It is me." Tears streamed down Priscilla's face. "I stand a better chance of remaining on the shelf than making a decent match… with the clothes Mama has insisted on making me wear and the musicales she insists we perform. There are jokes about me. I've heard them. I planned to buy a small cottage and find a job as a governess or companion, so I don't impair Rose's and Jane's chances of finding a match." Now the tears broke free.

Her grandmother's brows knitted together. "Young lady, I cannot imagine what possessed you."

"I needed... *independence*." Priscilla fought the urge to scream as the walls seemed to close in on her.

"I see. Here, you need this."

She accepted the lace muslin her grandmother handed her and wiped her nose. *But I've changed my mind. I still want independence, but it's not the same,* she thought.

"To be fair, your mother has, shall we say, turned over a new leaf. We should give her a chance to make amends, as she asks."

"I fear that Papa also knows of my gaming at the Lyon's Den, and I cannot imagine what he thinks."

"He may, but we haven't discussed everything," her mother said, startling them both as she entered the room. "Your father and I have a bridge or two to mend, and we are working on it. We both love you, Priscilla, but we would fear for your safety—and that of Mr. Smith."

Priscilla and her grandmother started, both turning their attention to the door.

"Who is Mr. Smith?" Grandmama asked with a slight catch in her voice.

Priscilla stood from the chair and walked to her armoire. Reaching deep inside, she withdrew a packet of clothes wrapped in twine. "*This is Mr. Paul Smith,*" she said with a contrite expression. A large muttonchop sideburn slipped from the package and fell onto the floor.

"*My stars!* What is that?" Grandmama asked, with one side of her mouth twisting into a smile.

"My sideburn."

"Goodness, we should burn that," Priscilla's mother said, "but you might need it once more—to apologize to Mrs. Dove-Lyon."

"I should. She put into place extraordinary measures just to ensure my safety."

"Of course, you must," Grandmama said. "And your mother and I will accompany you to the Lyon's Den, where we shall wait for you at the door, in our carriage."

"I agree. Your father would want you to apologize to the widow." Mother nibbled on her lower lip. "The widow told me you wanted independence. Do you still wish to leave us and find your own home?"

Grandmama remained quiet.

"Will you give me another chance, daughter?"

Priscilla tried to swallow past the lump in her throat. "I misjudged everything, Mama. I am sorry to have hurt you. And I have thought about doing something else with all the money I won."

"You say that like there is a great deal of money," Grandmama said.

Priscilla shrugged. "I think it's a lot. I would seed a loss here and there to encourage people, so they'd keep playing. When it counted, I won. However, after meeting Maggie and Penny, I thought a better use of my money would be for an orphanage. Maggie's story is tragic, and my heart hurts to think there are so many young girls and boys out there with no one that cares for them. And animals. Maggie was lucky to have found Penny. I think the animals provide something important that even an orphanage cannot."

"A dog or cat provides unfettered love," her mother said tenderly. "What a wonderful idea. Grandmama and I can organize fundraisers to help you. Although you still haven't told us how much you won."

"I haven't counted lately, but I think it's in the neighborhood of twenty thousand pounds." At her mother and grandmother's expressions, Priscilla reddened.

Her mother and grandmother fanned themselves simultaneously.

"That must go in the safe, for now, and quickly into a bank," her mother said in a loud whisper.

Priscilla stared blankly. "It's well hidden, but if I put it in our safe now, Papa will—"

"Pish! I will put it in *my* safe. But you must tell your father soon and have him help establish a bank account for you... *soon*," her grandmother said.

"Do you think Mr. Smith could be ready to go in an hour?" Mother asked. "Your father is busy all afternoon, and it's as good a time as any for your visit to the widow."

"I suppose you had help to get dressed," Grandmama said genially.

Priscilla nodded. Without a word, she rang the bell for Mary.

"I suspected as much. Don't worry about Mary, darling. I would have wished… But you left her no choice. She adores you, and this was as much my fault as yours, Priscilla." Mother kissed Priscilla's forehead before walking from the room with her mother-in-law.

Chapter Sixteen

Alex spent most of the night reading his father's last diary. Disturbing information from the book swirled in his head, taunting him, and forcing him to drift in and out of sleep. Even Mason had left the dark curtains in his room alone. He realized he needed to do something—anything. Now that he knew what had happened to his father, he had to act. It wasn't the worst information he had ever unearthed, but good grief! If his father had been poisoned, as he now suspected, he would have suffered greatly. The revelations he had gained from the diaries were worse than he had imagined and would be more difficult to navigate.

Heartbroken and bleary-eyed, he swung his feet over the side of the bed, resolved to face the day. Much of what he had read the evening before hung over him. There were things he needed to do. Montgomery had sent word that he would be there about eight o'clock, and Alex was certain Mason had sent word to the kitchen.

"Good morning, my lord. Your bath is ready, and your mother sent word asking you to break your fast with her." His valet quickly laid out his clothing.

"A good idea, Mason. A hearty breakfast is exactly what I need.

Ask Cook for some extra-strong tea. I was up rather late doing some research."

"I noticed the lights on in your study when I turned in," Mason said. "I figured to leave you alone and let you sleep longer."

"I only wish I had slept." Things Alex had read kept floating before him. His father had needed him, but he had been in France. His chest tightened.

Mason stoked the fire, warming the room. "Your mother has planned some visits and requested the larger carriage. So I had the smaller, unmarked one readied for you."

"Thank you. That's perfect for my needs." Alex planned to see Mrs. Dove-Lyon and meet Mr. Bennett. "I thought I saw Lord Montgomery ride up. Can you see him to the breakfast room?" He gathered his copy of the townhouse deed and the book he had been reading and went downstairs.

Alex opened the door to the breakfast room and found his brother, sister, and mother. At first, he had thought to mention his finds only to his mother, but that wouldn't be fair. He needed to protect all of them, and the only way to do that was to make everyone aware of what Papa's diary said.

"Good morning, everyone." All quieted, and he glanced from one to the other. "What?" he asked, suddenly feeling the focus of their discussion.

"Nothing, darling," his mother said. "Louisa and I were talking about the play last evening. She brought up that the lines seemed like they didn't belong to Shakespeare. I had noticed it as well."

"That was unfortunate. I hope Lady Priscilla enjoyed it. She loves Shakespeare. Perhaps I'll find out."

"Do you plan to see her today?" his mother inquired.

"I… am not sure. I spent most of my night poring over Father's last diary, and it is what I wanted to speak about with everyone today." He'd like to see Priscilla, but he felt the contents of the diary were more urgent. It was only thoughts of her that had soothed his restless mind and allowed him to sleep.

His mother placed her cup on the saucer and looked up. "What did you find, Alex?"

"If you don't mind, I'd like to wait for Montgomery. He sent word that he had learned something as well."

"That seems reasonable," Thomas said. "Hopefully, he has word from Bennett." Glancing between their mother and Alex, he flashed his brother a questioning look.

There was little opportunity to address his concern. Mother was there, and there would be no opportunity to parse the information. Besides, Alex felt sure she needed to hear what Father had to say.

Deciding against a heavy meal, he chose several pieces of toast, bacon, and a cup of Earl Grey tea. That might help wake his body.

The door opened, and Montgomery appeared. "Good! I've not missed the food!" he said cheerfully, rubbing his hands together.

The man was never in a bad mood—no matter the circumstances. Alex liked that about his friend. "We were waiting for you, hoping to hear your news, as well as what I have gathered." He pointed to the sidebar. "Make yourself at home."

"Don't mind if I do! My ladies," Montgomery said, giving a respectful nod to Alex's mother and his sister, who remained seated. In short order, he filled his plate and sat down. After a few bites, he said, "I heard from Bennett yesterday, and he thinks there's been a development. A runner saw Anders coming and going from Marble's room at the theater."

"This is great," Alex said.

"This is the first they've been seen together in a while," Montgomery continued. "We think there's a connection between Anders and the attempted robbery. Anders appeared angry when he left. Bennett said he tried to follow but lost him in a dark alley. Bennett is sure Anders and Mrs. Marble know they are being watched."

"What has Mrs. Marble to do with Papa?" Louisa asked.

Alex noticed his mother's face go pale at the question. "Rumors have circulated that Papa had a mistress. But based on what I've found, Mother, I believe that is untrue. Father loaned Lord Anders money for some sort of business venture, and I'd have to have more details about the business, but I suspect that venture didn't fare well. In Father's hand, he writes he met with Anders and his half-sister, Mrs. Delores Marble.

"At some point, Marble propositioned him and, when that failed, offered him wine. He commented he felt odd after drinking wine in her presence and couldn't account for why she was there. But I believe his entries disprove any notion of a mistress. I noticed this type of notation more than once."

He heard his mother let out a long breath.

"It leads me to believe that she may have bamboozled him out of money. When I took over his estate, it was badly in debt—showing huge expenditures, but with no notation of where the money went. With no trail, I could only follow the rumors, which led to Marble."

His mother inhaled sharply. "So, do you feel there was some sort of poison?" she said, then shook her head in disbelief. "Your father was an astute judge of character. And I never knew him to visit the theater without me. He just... wouldn't. I don't understand why she was involved with him."

"It has something to do with Anders, but I haven't worked out the details," Alex said.

Montgomery dabbed at his mouth and set down his napkin. "Bennett met with Anders's footman."

"The one in Newgate?" Thomas asked.

"Yes. He told Bennett that Anders and Marble had a routine involving bilking others out of money. He said Anders had promised him a bonus if the robbery had been successful—more if he killed Alex."

His mother and sister let out a collective gasp.

"We had them locked up and transported to prison, awaiting trial," Montgomery said. "I told Bennett we would be back to see him today."

"Mother, if you are all right with it, I'd like to show Bennett these entries," Alex said.

She nodded but then looked away, obviously pained.

"Thomas, if you'd be here in my stead today, I would be most grateful. There's still a lot I don't know, but we should make sure Mother and Louisa are not alone in the house."

"I'll stay here," Thomas agreed. "As long as you let me know what you find."

"Of course." Alex looked at Montgomery. "If you are ready, we can go."

"I am," his friend said, then took one more bite of toast and washed it down with tea before wiping his mouth again. "Thank you for breakfast, Lady Wrotham."

"You are always welcome, Lord Montgomery. And thank you for updating my family. You and Alex be careful."

Alex noticed Louisa smiling sweetly in Montgomery's direction and made a mental note to discuss that with his friend.

An hour later, Alex and Montgomery entered Bennett's office, finding the Bow Street Runner poring over notes. He looked up and pointed to the chairs in front of his desk. "I think we've found something, although I need to put this together."

"That's good news." Alex took a seat and extracted the leather notebook from his coat pocket. "I've also found something, and I think it will help with that. My father kept a diary. Even I knew nothing about it."

"That *is* something. Could he have detailed any of the meetings with Mrs. Marble?" Bennett asked.

"Father did exactly that," Alex said, growing angry about it. "He also discussed feeling sick and disoriented several times in her presence."

"Did your father believe he was being poisoned?" Bennett looked at Alex, alarmed.

"Yes. I think he did."

"I wonder if we can find a witness. The odd thing is the relationship between Anders and Marble. They are half-siblings, but it seems unusual for those born on the other side of the blanket to *friend* the legitimate children. Don't you think?" Montgomery mused. He turned to Alex.

"I agree. What if Anders is using Marble? Perhaps to gain property. There's at least one person who might know, and he's in Newgate. Anders's former footman," Bennett said. "I planned to meet with him today and will let you know my findings."

"It's important to discover what these two are up to before anyone else is harmed," Alex said, pushing past a lump in his throat. He had been too late to help his father. Perhaps, had he been home, his father could have confided in him, and the two of them could have stopped Anders and Marble. *The woman was never Father's mistress.*

They strategized on questions for Anders's former footman, agreeing Bennett should be the one to interrogate him.

Before Alex and Montgomery left Bow Street, Montgomery pointed to the familiar office on the street over. "Let's see Kitterman before heading to Newgate. I didn't mention the Home Office to Bennett, but they may have information on Anders by now."

"Yes, I agree." Alex gave the direction to Williams. "I think we are getting close to uncovering the truth."

"Yes, and that could make Anders more dangerous."

"If you are asking me if I plan to gamble, the answer is no. However, I do plan to stop by Lyon's Den. The woman has an ear to the wind and knows a lot. She may have insights about Lord Anders and Mrs. Marble. If she does, I'd like to know what she knows."

They met Kitterman as he was locking his office and preparing to leave. "I had expected the two of you earlier today," he said, unlocking the office and ushering them inside.

"That was my fault. I spent most of the night poring through Father's diaries—something I only recently learned he kept," Alex replied.

"Find anything?"

"I did. My father wrote of feeling sick and disoriented when drinking something Marble had given him, and it is my belief she doused it with something to render him that way. My mother explained that before he died, Father had become more confused. She attributed it to age or his heart."

"It sounds suspicious. And you say he wrote this several times?"

"Yes. Throughout the last month or so of the writing. He doesn't say where the meetings took place, but I suspected in a restaurant. He liked to hold meetings downtown at the club or in a hotel restaurant."

"That would have been the perfect place for Mrs. Marble to douse his drink—if she did that—and then make it appear they were 'inappropriate' when he became confused. The hotel would only illuminate that purpose."

"Poor Father. He enjoyed the lunch meetings. He used the location because some people weren't as welcome or comfortable at the club. I suspect Anders used this knowledge when he involved Mrs. Marble, since they wouldn't have admitted her at the club."

"Here's what we've found out. Anders and Marble, as you already have discovered, are half-siblings. Montgomery had mentioned Bennett told you she was a by-blow but didn't know the parentage."

Alex nodded, and Kitterman continued.

"Her mother was a former governess in Lord Anders's house. Her mother's name was Miss Margot Blemins, although that's not important. But when the governess was discovered pregnant, Anders's mother, the *now* Dowager Countess Anders, fired her. Blemins turned to her sister's brothel for a place to live. It's near Covent Garden. Mrs. Marble has never married, and her real name is Delores Blemins. Sadly, her mother died of tuberculosis when Marble was twelve, and she left her in the care of her aunt." He shook his head. "This happens a lot. It's a tragic loss for a child when there is no other parent. Anyway, Blemins assumed the name Marble when she became involved in the theater." Kitterman studied the notes in front of him. "I see nothing else of note—except suspicions she might be tied similarly to a few other elderly members of the peerage."

"Did those men die?" Alex asked.

"Yes. I've checked into them all, and each died of a stroke or other heart ailment. And most had deteriorated into a mental confusion that their families attributed to age," Kitterman replied. He looked up. "You are the first to question it. If what you suspect is true, we could have a murderer on our hands."

"If she suspects we know, she may do something desperate," Montgomery interrupted.

"Very true. May I see the book?" Kitterman asked.

A chill passed through Alex, and at that moment, he realized this calculating woman had probably planned his father's death. He handed his peer the book, and Kitterman thumbed through it, stopping to read the pages Alex had marked with pieces of paper.

"It appears the deal he struck with Anders didn't do well. Something to do with steam engines in America," Kitterman said, continuing to read. "I'm hoping your father comments somewhere in here on how he was supposed to be repaid."

"There's an entry in a few pages. Anders asked for more time. That's about when Anders introduced him to Marble," Alex said.

"This book starts a few months before his death. There must be another one." Kitterman looked up, concerned. "Where are you keeping these books? We may have a killer and a peer with some level of involvement—this would be our best evidence. Nothing must happen to this." He handed the book back.

"It's as if Father is speaking from the grave." Alex shook his head to clear it.

Kitterman agreed. "Your father's sudden onset of symptoms is like that of arsenic poisoning—a poison very easy for a killer to gain possession of. I hope to discover that in her apartment."

"I've turned this over in my head. When my mother mentioned the existence of a diary, it surprised me, and I tore my father's study apart to find them. We found books dating back to before he and Mother married. He created a discreet place under the floor; never would I have found them if not for my mother." He recalled his mother mentioning the family Bible. "In my angst to read this last night, I forgot to check the family Bible for Anders."

"It's all incredible." Kitterman shook his head in disbelief. "We've already confirmed the relationship with Anders. He was a second cousin to your father—the son of your father's brother's son. So the relationship is distant. It doesn't mean he didn't tug on your father's heartstrings. I knew Lord Wrotham for his generosity."

"Then there is this, which is what ignited my pursuit of this woman," Alex said, withdrawing his copy of the townhouse deed. "Bennett plans to request to see her copy. It'll be a forgery, I'm certain. Father signed it over to me months before all of this began. Her copy won't have this transaction—therefore, she couldn't register it because his solicitors had submitted this one month before."

Kitterman nodded. "That's significant in this paper trail. Your father's diaries and the entries will be damning. I doubt she even imagined their existence. I mentioned your situation to the prince regent, who is most concerned. He was good friends with your father. I will update him. We will close the net on them—but in the meantime, stay on guard. You two realize what that means. I will post men around your property and have someone watching Marble until we can make an arrest."

"The sooner the better," Alex said.

"You mentioned going to the Lyon's Den. We should go before the place lights up for the evening," Montgomery prodded, standing up.

Kitterman stood. "That's a smart businesswoman—and she has the pulse of this town. Do you plan to update her?"

"Some. Just on Anders. I think he's dangerous, and while his crime is not repaying a loan, the man bears watching," Alex said. He tucked the deed inside his coat alongside the small diary.

Twenty minutes later, the small black carriage pulled alongside the blue building on Cleveland Row.

"We shouldn't be too long, Williams," Alex said, shutting the door.

"Yes, my lord. I will round the block and park behind that black carriage there," the driver replied, pointing to a large black carriage.

Alex squinted. There was an embellished B on the side of the carriage. "Is that Lord Burleson's carriage?"

"I'm more interested in the women sitting inside," Montgomery said, nodding toward an older woman in the carriage. "That looks like the dowager countess *and* the countess. This cannot be good."

"We'd like to see Mrs. Dove-Lyon," Alex told Titan, who stood sentry near the entrance.

"She's with someone right now," the man returned, expressionless.

"If it's the person who belongs to the carriage containing those women, we already know Mr. Smith's identity. We must see Mrs. Dove-Lyon. And I would like to catch Mr. Sm… Lady Priscilla before she leaves."

The escort looked him over for a moment. "Wait here."

"Mrs. Dove-Lyon, I placed you in an untenable spot, and I am here to apologize," Priscilla said, fighting the urge to scratch her right cheek where the glue itched and wondering how she had borne wearing these itchy sideburns.

"I take it your mother has made you aware she knows of your ruse, as she has paid me a visit," the widow said. She stood. "Come here, child."

Priscilla stood and walked to the settee, where the widow sat.

"Sit," she said, patting the brocade seat. "Your father and my husband were the best of friends. While I did not approve of your path, I did what I thought necessary to ensure your... future and safety. I hope you understand that."

Priscilla nodded.

"And your mother—she was doing what she thought was right as well. I can agree that it feels misguided, but she loves you." The woman reached over and squeezed Priscilla's hands.

"I understand. She spoke with us this morning. I believe she wants to change things," Priscilla said thoughtfully.

The widow tilted her head and smiled. "So, I take it you didn't come here today to play cards?"

"No. I only came to apologize and thank you for all your kindness and consideration. And to tell you I plan to do something different with the money I won—something that helps others. On my way home last week, I rescued a young girl named Maggie and her dog, Penny, from bullies that were trying to hurt them. Maggie has no home and hasn't since her mother died of consumption. She had no one—except the dog, who took care of her."

"I'd like to help," Mrs. Dove-Lyon said. "I know others that support orphanages. And they could be of help." She scribbled a name on a piece of vellum and handed it to Priscilla. "Mr. Henry Stanton is a solicitor in town. He has an excellent reputation. He knows the orphanages in town and may steer you."

"Thank you."

Titan knocked on the door and opened it. "I'm sorry to interrupt you and… Mr. Smith."

"It's all right, Titan. I appreciate all your help, but this is the last time Mr. Smith will be here."

Titan gave a half-smile and a nod. "Ma'am, you have a visitor that insists on seeing you while you have Mr. Smith here."

Mrs. Dove-Lyon drew herself up. "Are they both here?"

"Yes, ma'am."

"Send them in. Lady Priscilla, unless I miss my guess, my 'guest' would prefer to speak with you," she said, wearing a patient expression.

Titan showed Alex and Montgomery into the room.

"Lord Montgomery, would you join me in my anteroom for a drink? We can leave the door to this room open, so Mr. Smith won't be compromised," the widow suggested.

Montgomery grinned. "If you have some of that wonderful brandy, I'm more than willing. This has been a long, dry afternoon."

"I agree." She walked behind her desk and pushed a button, which opened a door that had seemed a part of the wall.

"I'll fill her in, Wrotham," he said, glancing back, leaving the door open as he left the room.

Once they were alone, Lord Wrotham turned to Priscilla. "You shouldn't be here, Lady Priscilla."

She started to acquiesce, but the thought of his telling her, rather than asking why she was there, irritated her. "You have no right to tell me that."

"I'm sorry. That sounded rather dictatorial. Let me try again." He paused. "I'm surprised to see you here… but happy."

Smiling, she looked up. "My mother and grandmother insisted, and they wanted me to be in disguise." She chuckled. "I think it was as much about seeing the disguise as protecting my reputation."

Alex looked back at the opened door leading to the anteroom. He stepped closer, pulled the mustache back, and kissed her lightly on the lips.

"I wonder if you would like to ride through Hyde Park with me, and then visit Gunter's tomorrow, as an alternative activity to this one." He smiled coyly.

"Lord... Alex, I would love to." Butterflies swarmed her stomach.

He rubbed his hands together excitedly. "Excellent! I'll pick you up at ten o'clock."

Lady Dove-Lyon reentered the room with Lord Montgomery. "We should let this young lady get back to her carriage. Titan told me her mother and grandmother are waiting." She turned to Priscilla. "Please tell them I appreciated the visit. And I'm glad things appear to be working out."

"We will leave with her. I believe Montgomery updated you," Alex said.

The widow gave a half-smile. "He did indeed. And I appreciate your confidence. I will make sure no one allows *him* in the Lyon's Den again. Thank you both." The widow pulled a cord, and Titan appeared. "They are all leaving, Titan."

"Yes, ma'am. I'll see them out."

NO ONE DETECTED the man across the street, watching. He stood behind a dilapidated section of fencing, dressed in black with a floppy, dark hat covering much of his face. Slowly, he emerged from the alley between the stable and a white stucco building across the street and positioned himself to better advantage.

Anders watched the footman open the door to the larger front carriage and saw the young card shark, Mr. Smith, climb inside. Then Lord Wrotham and Lord Montgomery climbed into the smaller, unmarked carriage waiting behind.

"Curious," he muttered, observing the large, embellished B on the side of the first coach. Suddenly, he slammed his open hand against his forehead in annoyance. "Of course! *He* is *she*," he crowed. *Burleson's daughter is a redhead! How could I have been so blind?*

The second carriage jolted forward, turned left, and rolled down Cleveland Row, and the second carriage followed. Stepping from his hiding place, he leaned against the fence. There was a young woman there with red hair, Delores had told him. His face twisted into a malicious smile. "What an unexpected turn of events!"

Chapter Seventeen

The next day

PRISCILLA ROSE WITH the first light, glad to see the blaze of the fire in her fireplace and feel its warmth. Sitting up, she swung her feet over the side of the bed. Feeling her slippers, she pushed her feet inside, enjoying the warm fur against her skin, and scurried to do her ablutions. If she planned to keep her promise to Maggie *and* be back when Alex arrived, she needed to hurry.

Seeing her reflection in the looking glass above her sink, she paused and made a funny face. "Whoever invented these must have had a sense of humor!" she mused out loud.

"Ah, my lady, that they did… and a need to view their countenance," Mary added cheerfully, coming up behind her. "Your mama had this lovely riding habit made for you. She sent word to Madame Soyeuse yesterday afternoon, requesting she make one for you. The modiste delivered this a few minutes ago."

Wiping her hands on the linen towel, Priscilla walked to the wardrobe where the maid had hung the riding habit and fingered the green merino cloth. Embroidered around the bust and cuffs, it had fastenings on the back of the shoulder. A white double ruffle of Vandyke lace, set off by a moss silk shirt collar, enhanced its dressy appearance. On her bed, Mary placed a small beaver hat of green moss silk with matching kid boots and gloves.

"It's lovely," Priscilla said. "Madame has quite outdone herself. What did Mama say?"

Mary laughed. "I didn't hear her comments, but I was told Madame Soyeuse has orders for three like it, in different fabrics and colors—one for your mother, grandmother, and Jane."

Priscilla smiled. "I've seen nothing that compares to this. I love it."

"Well, we have dallied long enough. You need to get ready. That handsome lord will be here promptly at ten o'clock, if his past performance is any sign."

The door opened, and Rose and Maggie, Rose's new best friend, entered with Penny in tow. "We're ready. Papa said he picked out the gentlest of horses for us," Rose exclaimed.

Priscilla started to reprimand them for bursting into her room without knocking, but the smile on the dog's face caught her off guard. "Is Penny *smiling*?" she asked.

"Oh yes, m'lady. She speaks with her face. 'Tis one o' the best things about her," Maggie responded.

"Lady Priscilla will be down in about ten minutes," Mary said. "You two young ladies take yourselves, and Penny here, downstairs to break your fast. Lady Burleson will look for you both in the breakfast room." The girls left as quickly as they entered, with Penny right behind them.

"I've never seen Rose this excited. She treats Maggie as she would a sister," Priscilla observed.

"That's true, my lady." The maid was silent while she finished Priscilla's hair, tucking one long curl behind an ear and letting several others frame her face. "I think I have fixed it so that it looks elegant but will stay pinned."

Someone tapped at the door, and Jane poked her face in. "Do you mind if I join you?" She stepped inside. "You look beautiful, Cilla. Green agrees with you. Mama has become obsessed with redoing your wardrobe, and I heard Papa tell her to update our wardrobes as she saw fit." She nodded at her sister's riding habit. "Naturally, I asked for one of these. Maybe not the same pattern, but it's quite beautiful. It could be a traveling dress."

Priscilla turned and smiled at her sister. "I don't know what to make of Mama's new attitude, but I share in your delight. If you're ready, let's grab breakfast and head to the stable. I think it'll be fun to help Maggie ride her first horse. It was kind of Papa to purchase two ponies for the younger girls, and it's supposed to be a complete surprise."

"All they know is the groom has agreed to allow her to ride around the ring on what he thinks might be a gentle horse."

The sisters giggled as they walked downstairs.

"I am also glad you have stopped wearing sideburns. That was never a good look for you," Jane said with a snort.

Priscilla swatted playfully at her. "I've decided to use my winnings to create an orphanage; I still must work out the details. Grandmama put my money in her safe—until I discuss all of this with Papa. She knows the man that Mrs. Dove-Lyon said to call and is going to arrange a meeting."

"That's exciting," Jane said. "Do you have a location in mind?"

"Truthfully, I haven't thought it through. But I'd love your input, dear sister. It would be great fun to do something together," Priscilla said.

"I'm not sure Mama will allow us—or you—to run it... women in business and all that sort of thing. But then, it's impossible to expect what Mama would allow, since she's undergone a complete personality change these last few days." Jane lowered her voice conspiratorially. "Be careful what you say around Rose," she warned. "I've noticed she repeats everything she hears to Mama."

"Yes… it could be her age, but I think she sees it as orienting Maggie to the family."

"But the child isn't a member of the family. Surely she understands that," Jane said.

Priscilla hoped that she would find a family for Maggie somehow. She did not know how to go about that but would try her best. But that was worrying about tomorrow. Today, she would see Alex and couldn't wait for that. "Let's hurry the girls along, or I won't have time to see Maggie and Rose, and I'd hate to miss her first time on a horse."

Within twenty minutes, the four girls crossed the mews to arrive at their stable and found Lord and Lady Burleson already there. "How did you get here before us?" Priscilla asked, stunned to see her parents waiting for them.

Her mother looked at her father and smiled. "We had something we needed to take care of before everyone arrived. We have been holding this surprise for Rose and Maggie for days—and we couldn't believe it when Maggie asked about learning to ride. There was no way we wanted to let this opportunity go." She gripped her husband's arm affectionately.

Priscilla had never seen her mother so cheerful, but these last few days had changed her.

She looked up and saw the stable master leading out two ponies. The white ponies had only one visible difference, besides their gender. Rose's female pony had a small, brown, heart-like shape between her eyes. Priscilla couldn't believe her parents had done all of this for Maggie, the little urchin she had brought home only days ago.

"Woo… woo!" Penny wailed, doing her best to steal attention.

"I'm sorry, Penny, but unless there's a cart attached, you'll have to wait," Priscilla said, scratching the dog behind the ears. "Sweet girl."

"All right, girls… it's time to ride," her father said. He turned to Priscilla and Jane. "One of us will stay with Jane, who has agreed to watch the two girls. Lord Wrotham will be here shortly."

"I'll be back a little later, Rose," Priscilla said, kissing her sister. "Take it slow—especially you, Maggie."

"You look lovely, Priscilla," her mother said. "Would you mind if I saw you off with Lord Wrotham?"

For a second, Priscilla made sure the woman with her was the one she had always called *Mama*. "Of course, Mama. We should return now."

"It would be quicker to enter through the kitchen," her mother suggested, guiding her daughter toward the rear of the house. "We should be in the parlor before your guest arrives."

Priscilla's thoughts returned to the kiss at the theater, sending her pulse racing. He'd be there in a few minutes, and they'd be riding… alone. Would it be too much to hope for another kiss?

THE WOMAN TAPPED the roof of the hackney with her black parasol. "Stop here," she said in a gravelly voice, as the coach moved to the corner just beyond the Burleson townhouse.

Stepping from the coach, she fished in her reticule for the coin to pay the driver.

"Thank you, miss," the driver said, tipping his hat and accepting payment before driving away.

The empty hackney ambled down the street while she stood quietly and observed.

"This isn't what I expected so early in the morning. Much too much activity," she muttered from behind a dark veil that concealed much of her face. Quickly, she scanned the surrounding homes. "This is too easy," she murmured.

Paying careful attention, she waited until two coaches had passed before slipping across the street to the home three doors down from Burleson's house. Following the house's narrow driveway, she stayed close to the large shrubs that separated the property from the home next to it, crossing over to the mews. "Unless I miss my guess, the stable should be vacant," she mused.

Seeing no one in the stable, she found an unsecured door, entered… and checked around. "This will be perfect." The Burleson townhouse towered over the adjacent ones. "Five stories, no less! Plenty to work with," she sneered. "Soon I'll be closer to getting everything I've got coming to me!"

She arrived in the front just as a man on a horse arrived at the house. *I didn't expect Lord Wrotham to arrive. No matter. It'll be worth the wait, even if patience isn't one of my virtues.*

Undoubtedly, he's here for Lady Priscilla, and it appears the family is outside having some sort of tender family moment—a fortunate development for me. She cackled, enjoying the sound of her own wicked laughter. *It makes sense to wait inside, avoiding this frigid weather.* Feeling her gun in her pocket, she cast a wicked smile in the direction of the footman who stood holding horses, and made her way toward the Burlesons' servant entrance.

Chapter Eighteen

Alex couldn't believe he was getting time alone with her. Almost. Burleson had mentioned a footman would follow at a distance. He was taking no chances with his daughter.

But Alex had no objection and handed his horse's reins to the footman. "I'll be back, Traveler," he said, giving his horse a quick rub on the nose. Then he took the townhouse steps two at a time before using the ornate lion knocker.

"Good morning, Arlington. I'm here to see Lady Priscilla."

"Lady Priscilla is with Lady Burleson in the parlor, my lord," Arlington returned. "Please follow me."

Arlington announced Alex, and at the sight of Priscilla, he felt his mouth go dry. The last time he had seen her, she had been wearing those ridiculous, bushy sideburns and a mustache. She was beautiful. He gave an elegant bow. "Good morning, Lady Burleson, Lady Priscilla."

"Good morning, Lord Wrotham." Lady Burleson gave a casual wave toward the window. "The sun is shining. You picked the perfect day to ride Rotten Row."

"It's nippy but nice. Quite a pleasant start to the day," Alex agreed.

"Roberts will follow at a discreet distance. He should be out front with the horses," the countess said.

"I've made plans to stop at Gunter's for chocolate, so our outing may run a little longer," he said. "Will that be acceptable?"

Priscilla nodded. "It is, my lord."

A smile creased his face. "Are you ready?"

"I am," she said, and accepted his arm.

Her touch sent a delicious feeling skittering across his shoulders—a feeling unique to this woman. Never could he recall having felt anything comparable to it—except for the day his father presented him with Traveler, his beloved horse. Traveler had been to the Continent and back with him; they were inseparable, and the horse had on more than one occasion saved his life. Of course, he wasn't comparing this woman to his horse, but she evoked the same feeling of possessing something so cherished by his heart. Had his heart become involved with this woman in such a short period?

They mounted the horses and slowly made their way to Bond Street.

Alex could tell Priscilla wanted to say something but seemed hesitant. "What is it, Priscilla?"

"This ride—our names will be in the gossip sheets…" she began, and then stopped.

"I realize that, and that's all right." He told the truth.

She nodded and gave a tentative smile before turning her attention back to the traffic.

Being linked to her no longer mattered to him, despite his having avoided the marriage noose all these years. After all, he had agreed to do this to keep her safe.

But that's not why you're still doing this. Priscilla… this wonderfully smart woman had flipped his world. Everything he had once believed in where women were concerned no longer concerned him. She had a keen mind, was beautiful and resourceful—he realized it went deeper than attraction. Priscilla enjoyed doing things that mattered, like saving a small child and her dog from bullies. Admitting to himself that he wanted to court her had changed his nightly dreams from taunting to approving.

At that moment, he thanked her mother for dressing her in horrid colors and making her sing with a horrible singing voice. Had Lady Burleson gone the more conventional route of launching her daughter at every eligible man, one of them would have snapped Priscilla up before Alex returned to London. The thought of her luxurious auburn hair with threads of golden highlights caused his body to tighten. He had dreamed about it—imagining it covering his pillows, and her looking up at him through shimmering lavender eyes.

"I expected the road to be more congested on a day such as today," commented Priscilla, shaking him from his reverie. A smile spread over her face, producing a single dimple on the cheek closest to him.

Alex answered with a soft laugh, "I thought I had memorized your face, Priscilla. And now I see you have a dimple. Will you never cease to surprise me?"

"I-I'm not used to such flattery, Alex. But I like yours."

He spotted a vendor on the corner and realized he had forgotten to bring flowers. Honestly, it had been so long since he had courted anyone. He would fix that later today. "There is something I should explain. Otherwise, I fear if you heard it from another, you might misunderstand."

She looked up at him. "Oh?"

Alex had ventured outside of what was comfortable, but this was important to him. He had given this much thought and was committed to honesty between them. Looking ahead, he was relieved to see they were crossing into Hyde Park, giving more privacy. He slowed Traveler and moved closer to her horse. "Priscilla, I rarely do things I don't want to do." He kept his voice low. "It rattled your father when he found out you were going to the Lyon's Den."

"He knows?" Her face flushed red.

So, the earl still had said nothing to his daughter. "Yes, he does," he said, holding her gaze. "And he asked me to help keep you safe. That meant spending time together, to which I readily agreed. At first, it afforded a safe avenue to court you, and I told myself it was a favor to Burleson."

Her lips formed a thin line, but she remained quiet.

"Somehow, that changed." Traveler neighed and snorted as if agreeing. "Ha! My horse knows me better than I know myself. You are special to me, and I cannot recall any other woman I could say that about. The kisses and caresses… and this outing… they were and are real. I *wanted* to be with you… from the first time I saw you at your parents' house party."

Her eyes brightened. "But the musicales… the *ton*'s gossip…"

"That matters not to me. I would be lying to say I'm not familiar with all of that, but the horrible musicales kept you unattached… and gave *me* the chance to meet you."

"I see," she said, swallowing hard. But her eyes never left his.

"Until this past year, and even now, I've been mired in my work and my father's affairs. Had it not been for orange dresses and dreadful songs"—he paused, smiling—"you may have married another peer and could have been out of my reach before we could have known each other." He reached over and touched her hand. "That would have been a loss—*my* loss."

Her lips formed an O. A moment later, she spoke up. "But you wouldn't have known… that."

"I assure you, I would have missed out on knowing you." They followed a branch of the Serpentine around a curve, and Alex checked over his shoulder to make sure the footman still followed. "You don't take compliments very well, do you?" It was more of a statement than a question.

"I suppose not," she admitted. "Mostly because I'm not used to getting them. They've always been for Jane."

"Perhaps your guilelessness makes you different."

They passed a small clearing, and Alex realized that, except for the footman, they were alone. The bulk of visitors had veered onto the wider park path, while they had taken the other one. "Do you know how to skip rocks?" he asked.

"You mean make them hop across the water? Papa tried to teach me as a child, but I never quite caught on."

He gave her a look. "Hard to believe. I halfway expect you're as proficient at that as you are at cards," he said, grinning.

After steering Traveler into a sunny clearing near the river, he slid down and tied the horse to a nearby bush. Reaching up to help her down, he indicated for the footman to move to the tree a short distance away but kept him in the line of sight. Roberts nodded and gave them some space.

Reaching down, Alex picked up two small pebbles, both smooth and about the size of his thumb. Leaning over, he took his rock and threw it, watching it skip five times across the water. "You try."

"This may be a waste of a perfectly good rock," she teased, but accepted the rock, turning it over in her hand. "You came closer to the ground, I noticed," she said, trying to copy what she had seen him do.

"Yes, now hold the rock flat and throw it with a hard flick of your wrist," he instructed.

She did as he explained, and it skipped once.

"I think there's a talent there. Would you mind if I showed you?"

They both glanced in Roberts's direction, but the man had leaned back against a picnic table and was staring into the water.

"I would like that," she said without hesitation, accepting another rock. "I can see where this could be addictive."

Alex stepped behind her and inhaled her fragrance while he gently gripped her right hand. "This is how your wrist must move," he said, showing her the way to flick the rock. She smelled delicious—like bergamot and lemons, fresh and captivating. He fought the impulse to bury his face in her hair. "Now try again."

She did, and it skittered seven times across the water.

"Seven times!"

"Beginner's luck," she said excitedly, clapping her hands in delight.

"If you say so," he teased.

"I promise. Papa will be thrilled when he learns I've learned! The difference must be going low to throw it."

A mix of pride and exuberance washed over him, and they each quickly gathered rocks to launch them.

"You are doing a fine job. If Mr. Gunter wasn't expecting us, I'd suggest a contest." *Maybe next time,* he thought. "We should go. Roberts is watching us, so I suppose his nap is over."

She burst out laughing. "I've noticed that before but would never tell Papa."

"A sleepy chaperone can be an advantage," he quipped with a wink. "Perhaps he will need another nap."

Helping her onto the horse, he noticed her healthy flush from riding in the chilled air. They returned to the path along the Serpentine and picked up the pace to Berkeley Square. "You truly enjoy riding, don't you?" he said.

"I do, and Nadia needs to be ridden. She gets bored in the stable, but I rarely get to ride her while in town."

"She's a beautiful bay with a lovely sounding name. What does it mean?" he asked, not missing the white crescent on the forehead of the bay.

"It's a Biblical name. It means hope. Years ago, my governess read the Bible story to us, and I became fascinated with the name. When Papa gave her to me a few years ago, I thought it was perfect for her." She leaned forward and rubbed the side of her horse affectionately.

As they pulled up to Gunter's, Roberts dismounted and caught their reins, while Alex helped Priscilla dismount.

"We are going inside to have chocolate. Is there something you'd like to have, Roberts? I'll make sure you get it."

"Thank you, milord. Anything they serve is a treat," the footman said.

"Yes, it is for us as well. See that they water the horses while you're waiting," Alex said.

"Yes, my lord. Right away."

Alex turned to Priscilla. "I've had my sights set on having some confection from Gunter's. How about you?"

"Definitely," she said, smiling and taking his arm.

The two of them went into the confectionary and were greeted by a server who led them to a small table off to the side.

"I fear all the eyes of the *ton* are on us," she said, keeping her eyes downcast.

"Oddly, I don't think so. The people at the table near us just got up and left. And the others that are coming in seem only interested in the food," Alex returned, handing her a small menu. "What would you like?"

"I'll have the chocolate and maybe a biscuit or two. Surprise me with the flavor."

He gave their order to the server. "The lady will have chocolate and whatever biscuits are the warmest. And I'll have a lemonade and the same biscuits."

The young man gave a quick bow. "Thank you, my lord."

A few minutes later, the man returned with their order and poured the chocolate into the cup for Priscilla.

It amazed Alex how comfortable it was to be with her. They talked about different things, including her unique talent for cards.

"I take it your father never mentioned that he knew about Mr. Smith," Alex said.

"No." She sighed in resignation. "It was bound to happen. Yet he has said nothing to me. I'm not sure how this happened, but Mama found out, and she has been a different person toward me—even having this riding habit designed for me. I have changed my thoughts regarding what to do with the money, though," she added.

"Really? To what?"

"After I rescued Maggie and little Penny, I decided to find a way to help children like Maggie."

"An orphanage?"

"Yes! But better. One that helps children learn to read and write and gives them a chance to learn skills that could elevate their station in life and keeps them away from workhouses. That could mean growing up to be a governess, a housekeeper, or even a doctor—vocations that are generally out of their reach as orphans. Mrs. Dove-Lyon gave me Mr. Roger Stanton's name. My grandmother knows his family well and plans to contact him for me."

He smiled. "That's an excellent use of your money. And I'm very well acquainted with Mr. Stanton. Let me know if I can be of help. Count on my mother and sister to help with any fundraising efforts." Alex reached over and put his hand over hers. "I hate so much to do this, but we should probably head back."

She nodded and looked around the room. "I've had no one do anything as lovely as this for me, Alex."

"That's a shame. We should change that," he said, giving her hand a gentle squeeze.

As they crossed back into Mayfair, Alex slowed down at a flower vendor and slid down from his horse. "Give me a minute," he said, handing his reins to Roberts, who had dismounted behind him and secured the horses.

"I have some lovely roses, my lord," the old woman said, pointing to a variety of colorful blooms.

"They are lovely, but I'm looking for something very specific." He glanced up at Priscilla as he perused the selection, until he saw the bouquet of white and green Lenten roses, with delicate sprigs of red berries and greenery. "I'll take those," he said, then paid the woman and carefully tucked the flowers in his saddlebag. Taking the reins, Alex mounted his horse.

When they arrived at the Burlesons' townhouse, the footman slid from his mount. "Shall I take your horse to the stable, my lord?"

"That might be best. I won't be long, but there are a couple of things I wanted to attend to," Alex said, sliding down from his saddle before assisting Priscilla. Reaching into his saddlebag, he withdrew the roses and took his cane from its holster on his saddle.

"Very good, my lord," Roberts said with a half-smile. "I'll take the horse to the mews with the others."

At the door, Arlington greeted them. "Lady Priscilla, Lord and Lady Burleson, and the girls are in the back." He smiled. "If you'll allow me to say so, my lady, those are the prettiest ponies I have ever seen. The girls are enchanted… especially Miss Maggie. You did her a big kindness."

"I suppose we should go to the back," Priscilla said. "Would you mind?"

"Of course not," Alex said, extending his arm. "I'm eager to see."

Chapter Nineteen

Priscilla couldn't recall a more perfect day. Just looking in his direction caused her heart to skip. And never had she imagined hearing a man tell her the things Alex had said today. He hadn't declared his love, but he had told her he cared for her, and had since they had met.

It was more than she had ever thought to hear from a man—not when her claim to fame had been causing extreme pain to their ears through what a gossip sheet once referred to as "caterwauling." She winced. Her mother had ordered the columnist fired; the editor—fearing a loss of subscribers—had obliged. Not a high point in her life. Not like today.

"Are those for me?" she asked finally, nodding at the bouquet.

His face reddened when he realized he was still holding flowers. "Not well done of me. I should have brought them this morning, but I realized on the way to the park that I had forgotten."

"They are beautiful," she said, accepting the bouquet. "You've probably noticed the white and maroon ones in the yard. Mama loves them."

"As does my mother. I wanted something that suited you, and

these have a quiet beauty that complements each other, but doesn't overpower."

"What a lovely way to describe them. Mama planted the gardens with summer varieties and Lenten roses, but these have a lovely winter bloom."

"Look, everyone! Cilla's back," Rose said, running to her sister, with Penny trailing behind. "You should see Maggie riding her pony!"

The three of them rushed to the stable, where Maggie was being led around by one of the stable hands. "Look at me, Rose. I'm on a horsey!" She giggled.

Penny bounded behind them in the ring. "Wooo... wooo!" she called, to the delight of the two girls.

"Look at me, too, Cilla!" Rose said, using the block to mount her pony.

"I cannot wait to see that." Priscilla looked down and remembered the flowers in her hand. "These beautiful flowers belong in a vase. I'm sure I can find one in the kitchen, and then I'll join you."

"Should I accompany you?" Alex asked.

Her heart filled just looking at him. She couldn't think of anything she'd like better than a chance to kiss this man in the privacy of... anywhere. Judging from the time, most of the staff would be in their dining area, eating. "That's unnecessary. There are vases in the kitchen pantry. I won't be long."

WHAT LUCK! THE staff was downstairs eating, and the intruder had the run of the house. As she edged out of the cold room, she peered out the small kitchen window. "This is my lucky day!" she said, watching her quarry coming toward her with flowers. "Excellent, little dove.

Just a little further," she said, backing into the pantry.

She watched Priscilla walk into the kitchen.

Priscilla searched around the sink area and in the small closet where the cook kept small containers. "Nothing here," she said, turning to go into the pantry.

"Woof!" The door opened, and Penny bounded into the room, almost prancing.

"Oh, you little darling," Priscilla said, kissing the dog on the head and scratching it behind its ears. "Let me put this in a vase, and I'll find you a treat."

"Wooo… wooo!" The dog hopped around excitedly.

From within the closet, the woman muttered, "When did gentlemen start allowing dogs in their kitchens?" She felt in her reticule and patted the bottle of laudanum. "Just a little closer."

PRISCILLA FOUND A pitcher of water. "Now, I need a vase." She walked into the closet, and someone grabbed her, slamming their fist into her face and pulling her the rest of the way inside. Dropping the flowers, she screamed and flailed against the person with every ounce of her strength, clawing at their head, and throwing jars and pots at the intruder.

"Grrrrrrr!" Penny growled and launched herself onto the person holding Priscilla. She clamped her jaws around the arm that held Priscilla and shook it furiously.

"Ow! Get your damn dog off me," shrieked the intruder in a man's voice, trying to shake the dog off and hold Priscilla at the same time. But the dog refused to let go. Instead, she became more vicious.

It was a man dressed as a lady. *But who?* Priscilla fought with everything she had. "Let me *go*," she yelled. She reached for a jar with her left hand and smashed it into his face, knocking his hair askew. And began clawing at his face.

Wedging her against the shelf and his side, the man forced her mouth open and shoved in a foul-smelling cloth with his free hand. Then he poured something in it, stuffing the wet rag further into her mouth. She nearly retched. *Laudanum*. Her words were muffled, and she struggled to breathe through her nose. "H-help me," she said with a cough, fighting the fog threatening to take her over. Her field of vision began shrinking.

"You are coming with me," the man growled, doing his best to shake off the dog. Frustrated, he dropped her for a minute and hit the dog, but Penny only held on, ripping at his arm.

Priscilla tried to pull the rag out of her mouth and crawl out of his reach, but she was growing weaker. She struggled against the effects of the drug, pulling on the rag, which seemed larger than she recalled. It was soaked with laudanum, and touching it sent more down her throat before she could stop it. Gripping it and gagging, she finally got it out and dropped it.

"Ow… umph… off me, damn dog… you're tearing off my arm!"

"Grrrrrrrrrrrr…"

"The commotion is in the kitchen," she heard Alex say as he slammed open the door. *Hold on,* she told herself.

Looking behind her, as if through pinholes, Priscilla saw a blonde wig fall off the man's head to reveal Lord Anders. He had visited her parents frequently. *Why was he doing this?* She could hear the dog growling and the man screaming.

"What the hell? Oh my God! Priscilla," Alex roared.

She saw Alex and his friend, Lord Montgomery, come into the room, throwing back things to get to her.

"Here, hold this at his chest, and run him through if he moves," Alex said, unsheathing his sword and passing it to his friend.

"Get the dog off me!" Anders screeched, his arm now dripping with blood.

"Shut up and count yourself lucky Montgomery holds my sword," Alex said.

She could barely hear Alex's voice.

The fog was thick and dark, and with only a pinprick of light, Priscilla could barely see. The last thing she saw was Alex's steel-gray eyes and his lips moving. He picked her up and held her close.

"Get a doctor!" Alex roared, holding Priscilla's blood-splattered, limp body. He ran through the hall from the kitchen, looking for the closest room he could find.

"I'm right behind you, my lord," her maid yelled. "Put her on the couch in here."

He laid Priscilla down on the parlor settee.

"Oh my God! Where's Priscilla?" Lady Burleson rushed into the parlor with her husband.

Alex looked up as Montgomery entered with her parents and her grandmother. "He has dosed her with God knows how much laudanum. There was an empty vial and a rag on the floor. We need a doctor." He covered her with a blanket. Leaning over her, he kissed her. "Please keep breathing, Priscilla. Stay with us," he murmured in her ear. He could feel her heart, but her breathing was shallow, and her pulse was slow. "Where is that doctor?" he cried out.

"Oh my God! My little girl," her mother screamed, pushing him out of the way.

Alex stood, understanding a mother's pain, while fighting back tears of his own. Had he insisted on going with Priscilla to the kitchen, none of this would have happened.

"Sit her up and try to make her walk. Keep her heart pumping," her father said from behind him. "Roberts should be back with Dr. Spencer any minute now."

Alex did as he was bidden and tried to quiet her moans. At least she *was* moaning. That had to be a good thing with all that drug in her system.

"Let me help with Priscilla until the doctor comes. Maybe you men can see to *Lord Anders*." Burleson fairly spat the name.

"Montgomery, I'm glad you showed up when you did," Alex said as they walked back to the kitchen. He wiped his face as the two men pulled Anders's bloodied and nearly unconscious body from the closet. They used rope that a stable hand brought them and bound the earl's legs and hands as tight as they could, leaving the injured arm loose. "I don't think he'll ever use that mangled arm again." He saw the deep scratches on the man's face and knew Priscilla had fought for her life.

They heard the front door open and Arlington escorting the doctor to the parlor. Alex took a deep breath. "Hand me that empty jar, Montgomery," he said, spotting the wet rag and the nearly empty vial near them. "Without Anders telling us, we've no way to know how full the vial was."

"I see where you are going," Montgomery said. "If Dr. Spencer can ring out this rag, maybe he can get an idea of how much he forced into her."

Dr. Spencer was already working with Priscilla, pleased he could get her to mumble a word or two.

"We brought you the cloth Anders used to pour the laudanum into her. We thought if you could squeeze it into this jar, you might have a better idea of how much she took," Alex said.

"Great idea," the doctor said.

"I'll do it," Mary volunteered.

When he studied the still-wet rag and considered the amount

drained from it, a look of relief spread over the doctor's face. "She probably saved her own life when she pulled the rag out. And sitting her up and walking her around probably helped, too."

"Thank goodness she's a fighter," Priscilla's mother said, kissing her on the cheek and giving way to a few snickers that cut through the tension.

Feeling untold relief that she would make it, Alex put his arm on Montgomery's back. "Thank you, my friend. I'm glad you're here—but *why* are you here?"

"I first tried your house, but Mason said you were here, and I had to find you. Kitterman sent word that they had discovered Anders's involvement with other men that Marble had tricked out of property. The two were working together. Weirdly, a hackney driver reported an odd fare from this morning to Bow Street. He said a man dressed as a woman had him drop him off in Mayfair. He was certain it was a man. When Bennett saw the address, he sent word to me to find you. We suspected Anders. Your father's diary mentioned a loan to Anders for fifty thousand pounds—an investment in steam engines in America, I believe."

"Whew! That's an enormous loan. So unlike Father to do that."

"The investment was mismanaged, and Anders lost the money. Your father's diary mentioned he asked for an extension the day he introduced him to his half-sister, Delores Marble."

Alex recalled the entries his father had written about feeling drugged and sick. Had he come home earlier, perhaps he could have stopped this and saved his father.

"I know what you are thinking, and you should stop that. You couldn't have known. None of this was your fault," Montgomery said, laying his hand on Alex's back. "Meanwhile, Kitterman had considered the properties she gained and found that all the owners died before she received their property—each time, with a deed signed over to her. And in each case—until your father's situation—the family accepted their loved one died of natural issues and didn't draw attention to it."

"Arsenic poisoning?" Alex asked.

"That's what Kitterman suspects, and Bennett agrees."

"That's hard to prove unless you find the arsenic in her possession," Alex noted.

"It seems both brother and half-sister had their agendas but were working together. You were right about the deed for the townhouse. It was a forgery. Bennett asked to see hers and took it to your father's solicitor this morning for signature comparisons. They weren't a match to your father's. The woman is being arrested, and if they find arsenic in her possession, she will probably hang."

Alex leaned down and picked up items on the floor of the pantry. "Here's a dark veil and a rather ugly blonde wig. It looks like he was setting up Delores. You recall one of the men that held us up mentioned *she*, and when Bennett interrogated the man, he said that he couldn't see the woman's face, only the blonde wig." He shook the wig. "But I don't understand why."

"Where is Priscilla?" Lord Burleson asked, returning.

"She's resting on the settee in your parlor. Mary is with her," Alex said, running his hand through his hair. "My God! Anders poured laudanum down her throat, so she was out. Maggie's dog, Penny, nearly severed the man's arm and showed no signs of letting him leave with Priscilla. Montgomery and I pried her jaws off him."

"Thank God you got to her in time. I cannot allow myself to think what would have…" Burleson let the words die as he walked over to Penny and petted her on the head. "Arlington," he called.

The butler appeared out of nowhere. "Yes, my lord."

"Bring me a bucket of soapy water and a towel. This dog defended my daughter and probably saved her life. And I'm going to make sure she's cleaned up," Burleson said. "And gets a good meal."

"If it is all the same to you, my lord, it would honor me to do that for you," Arlington said, stooping down and checking Penny's face.

"No cuts, but her face is sore to my touch. I believe he punched her. Her eye is swelling."

"Woof," Penny barked. Her energy was depleted, and she was lying on the floor, panting.

"Have the doctor look at her once he checks out my daughter," Burleson said, petting her.

"She is a sturdy animal. The man's arm will probably have to be amputated," Alex said.

"He won't need it where he's going," Bennett said, entering the room. The Runner surveyed the bloody mess in the kitchen. "I'm sorry it took us so long to get here. I've been interrogating Mrs. Marble, but we can discuss that later."

"I'll leave this to you two, if you don't mind. I'd like to check on Priscilla." Alex walked into the parlor, where her grandmother, sisters, Maggie, and Lady Burleson surrounded her.

"My dog didn't let 'im take 'er," Maggie said proudly.

Alex gave the little girl an affectionate hug. "We are so glad she was here."

Mrs. Smithers, the housekeeper, walked in behind him. "We've put everything to rights, my lady. That was some kind of struggle in there." She turned to Alex. "Thank you, my lord, for saving our dear Priscilla."

"I arrived almost too late." A chill passed through him with those words. "Penny saved her. That dog would have given her life for Priscilla. There was no way she was letting the man out of that kitchen—not with both arms, at least. He will probably need an amputation."

"They could persuade me to yank the rest of it off," Mary said tersely. "I've never wished ill for someone, but that man's the devil."

"The important thing is, she will survive this," Dr. Spencer said, standing up and closing his bag. "Let her sleep here, and then move her into her room a little later. I'll check on her this evening." He looked at Alex. "From what you describe, the man's arm will have to come off."

"He's been bound and moved to Bow Street. Go there," Lord Burleson said. "I don't want that man in my home one minute more."

Epilogue

Three weeks later

"Mother, this elaborate dinner tonight is much more than Priscilla or I need," Alex murmured from behind his morning newspaper.

"What?" Lady Wrotham dropped her gossip sheet and stared at him. "You agreed!"

"I'm kidding. Priscilla and her family are looking forward to it," he said. "I only wanted to get a rise out of you."

"Pish! I was a young girl once upon a time. Every young girl needs a splashy engagement announcement. Besides, it'll be my first party in quite a while, and it's right that she be welcomed into the family."

He laid the paper down. "Isn't that what the bridal celebration does?"

Louisa set down her fork and snickered. "A party will be nice, and it'll give Thomas a chance to meet some ladies!"

Thomas choked from across the table. "Leave me out of this. I'm content to attend, as a guest, but I have no interest in the parson's noose."

"Thomas, that's vulgar," his mother reprimanded him. "Be careful, or I will ship you back to school for the holidays."

Alex hooted.

"Seems like only a month ago that you were also avoiding the same, dear brother," Thomas taunted him.

"True… but then I met Priscilla, and there is only one of her." Alex smiled. "And if I didn't scoop her up, someone else would have. I couldn't have that."

"And is Jane like her?" his mother asked before leisurely taking a bite of toast.

"She is compliant on the outside, but full of mischief inside," Alex said. "As her new brother-in-law, I will take a special interest in helping to secure her a suitable match."

Rustling of the paper from the end of the table told him he had hit his mark. Jane was only sixteen, but he noticed his best friend's interest whenever she entered a room. Time would tell.

"Thomas, I have a few errands on Bond Street, but I'll be back soon and challenge both of you and Montgomery to billiards today, while we leave last-minute preparations for Mother and Louisa."

Both men agreed, and Alex and Montgomery set off to the jeweler's on Bond Street.

"You've waited for the last minute with this one, Alex," Montgomery said.

"Nonsense. I commissioned the ring weeks ago, and the jeweler promised it ready today."

"I'm still astonished by this transformation. You are happy about being engaged," Montgomery said. "I wish I could have predicted this. I'd have put it in the book at White's!"

"Not funny. I think almost losing her made me realize my feelings—and once I did, there seemed no use in putting off the engagement." It seemed like forever since he had first seen Priscilla pretending to be a man and playing cards at the Lyon's Den—the same place he had used to replenish his family's coffers and move on from the fallout of his father's illness and death.

"Let's get this done, so I can show you and Thomas how to lose at billiards," he said, causing them both to laugh.

The engagement dinner

"IT'S SO THOUGHTFUL of Lady Wrotham to include Rose and Maggie at the dinner party," Priscilla said, walking up the steps to the Wrotham townhouse. She looked up at the six-story structure in front of her. It sprawled almost the entire block and appeared more like a mansion than a townhouse. "Alex told me she planned a small table for them in a nearby area. The governess is to dine with them."

"That will make them both feel special," Lady Burleson said, taking a deep breath as they reached the top of the steps. "I had forgotten how grand this place is."

The door opened, and Hartford stepped aside. "Welcome to Wrotham Place, Lord and Lady Burleson, Dowager Countess Burleson, Lady Priscilla, Lady Jane—and you must be Lady Rose and Miss Maggie."

"Thank you, kind sir. You got my whole family right," Maggie said. "I would have brought my dog, Penny, but Father Burleson told me there would be a special dinner for her."

Lady Burleson laughed softly. "She will soon want to be called Queen Penny."

"Yes, my lady," Hartford said, trying to swallow a laugh. "She's quite the heroine. Please follow me."

Priscilla beamed, thinking back to when she had stopped her hackney to bring the child and her dog to safety. Whatever had possessed her that day, it had been the right thing to do. She could never regret it. Her parents had adopted Maggie, making her part of their family.

"Ah, darling, there you are," Alex said, walking up to Priscilla and placing a kiss on her cheek. "Mother is eager to see everyone. They are waiting in the drawing room."

As they entered the drawing room, the number of guests who had already arrived astonished Priscilla. Among the many there to celebrate her and Alex's engagement included Mrs. Dove-Lyon, who stood with Lord Henry Stanton, the Earl of Egerton, and his wife, Lady Olivia.

"Ah! There she is," Lord Stanton said. "We were just discussing you, Lady Priscilla. Allow me to introduce my brother, Mr. Roger Stanton, one of London's finest solicitors. I say that because we understand you will need help with establishing an orphanage."

Mrs. Dove-Lyon stepped forward. "I can vouch for the man. He and his brother quickly became two of my favorite patrons." She leaned closer to Priscilla and whispered, "Much like your dear Mr. Smith, Lord Wrotham, and Lord Montgomery, it was their personalities more than their contributions to my coffers." A smile creased her face beneath the veil.

Priscilla owed Mrs. Dove-Lyon a debt of gratitude.

Roger Stanton stepped forward. "It is my pleasure to meet you and be of help. It's no secret among this group that I was once an orphan, and therefore, I am interested in doing anything I can to help them."

"That would be wonderful. Perhaps you will meet with my sister, Jane, and me to discuss designs and functions for the building. Jane has agreed to help me with the project."

"Did I hear my name?" her sister asked, walking up on the arm of Lord Montgomery.

It didn't miss Priscilla's notice that Lord Montgomery had shown up the day after Anders's arrest to check on Jane and Priscilla. She'd also noticed her mother wasn't promoting either one of her daughters to the handsome lord, something that only a few weeks ago would have been totally unlike her.

"It would be my pleasure. I will reach out to you later this week and secure a date." The man smiled broadly to both she and Jane, who had walked up beside her, holding Lord Montgomery's arm. Priscilla couldn't help but notice the look on Lord Montgomery's face. Her sister was truly a beauty.

"It was quite unnerving to find out what Lord Anders had done," Lady Olivia Egerton said, jolting Priscilla from her musings.

"Indeed," Roger Stanton agreed. "The prince regent is most distressed over the death of Lord Wrotham—and with Anders's apparent ties to it. For now, they have locked him in the Tower, but he may find himself at the end of a noose. His half-sibling, Mrs. Delores Marble, has already been found guil—I apologize for my crassness. I should never have spoken thus with ladies present."

"Not at all. After what the man and his sister put our families through, we have no qualms about discussing their fate," Priscilla said evenly.

"You are certainly right, my dear daughter," Lord Burleson said. "Her mother and I have never in our lives felt more powerless." He smiled at Priscilla. "In more ways than one!"

"I believe you and Lord Wrotham are evenly matched in this betrothal," Mrs. Dove-Lyon said sweetly. "He will value you as his helpmate."

Lady Wrotham accepted a spoon from Hartford and tapped her glass, making a light, clear ringing sound. "It is almost time for dinner. But my son, Alex, has a few words for Lady Priscilla."

Alex walked from his mother to Priscilla wearing the biggest smile she had ever seen.

He dropped to one knee, withdrew a small velvet box from his waistcoat pocket, and took her hand. The entire room was hushed.

"Lady Priscilla Burleson, I know I've asked this before, but I wish to ask it again in front of these witnesses."

Priscilla bit her bottom lip nervously, anticipating the usual bout of anxiety at being the center of attention. But nothing happened. Relieved, she smiled.

"Will you do me the honor of becoming my wife and making me the happiest of men?"

Priscilla met his eyes and blinked back tears. "I will."

He opened the box and withdrew a gold, amethyst, and diamond ring, and slipped it on her finger. "The diamonds and gold were part of my mother's wedding ring. Mother and I both felt Father would want you to wear them. He would have loved you." Alex's eyes glistened. "I added the amethyst as a symbol of the love I feel for you."

"You love me?" she whispered. He had never said that.

"I do... love you, Priscilla. The moment I met you, I couldn't get you out of my head. It went against everything I thought I wanted. And I realized I wanted so much more than I knew. I wanted you." He pulled her up to him and leaned in for a kiss.

She couldn't get enough of this man. Surely everyone around her could hear her heart, as it felt like it would pound out of her chest. Alex's gentle hands cradled her head, and he leaned in for a deep kiss.

Someone coughed in the background. "Save that for the honeymoon, Wrotham," Montgomery whispered from behind.

Blushing, she pulled back, breaking the kiss, but didn't take her eyes off her fiancé.

"Love is precious. Cherish your lives together," Grandmama said, wiping her eyes.

"This is what I wish for all of my daughters—all four of them!" Priscilla's father added, hugging his wife.

"If you will excuse my fiancée and me for a few minutes," Alex said. "I'd like to say a little more."

He walked her to the terrace and drew the curtain behind them. "I meant everything I said in there. You have my heart, Priscilla. I almost lost you, and had that happened, I cannot think I would have ever been the same. From the first day I met you…"

She put a gloved finger to his lips. "I could not get your image out of my head, either. I think I fell in love with you the first night I met you. Certainly, you had my heart at that first kiss—the memory of which I shall enjoy until the day I die."

"Not to change the subject, but did you know the crest for my family is a lion?" he asked with a sly grin, pulling a small brown pouch from his coat pocket. "I thought it apropos that you have a small pin of our family crest, as much to welcome you to the family as to mark the place that threw us together." He pulled out a small gold lion pin with amethyst and diamond chips and pinned it on her breast. Its simple elegance matched her lavender silk dress. "I had forgotten that. Well, then! Truly, I have found a lion of my own."

Priscilla slanted her lips and kissed her fiancé. His lips were warm and soft, allowing her tongue to slip inside. Wrapping her hands around his neck, she gently tugged him closer, twining her fingers in his hair. His hands drifted down her sides, and both were breathing heavily as their lips moved together.

"I think this wedding cannot come too soon," he murmured against her lips.

"Not much longer, my darling lion!" she said with a playful growl.

~Not the end ~

About the Author

Anna St. Claire is a big believer that *nothing* is impossible if you believe in yourself. She sprinkles her stories with laughter, romance, mystery and lots of possibilities, adhering to the belief that goodness and love will win the day.

Anna is both an avid reader author of American and British historical romance. She and her husband live in Charlotte, North Carolina with their two dogs and often, their two beautiful granddaughters, who live nearby. *Daughter, sister, wife, mother, and Mimi*—all life roles that Anna St. Claire relishes and feels blessed to still enjoy. And she loves her pets – dogs and cats alike, and often inserts them into her books as secondary characters. And she loves chocolate and popcorn, a definite nod to her need for sweet followed by salty…*but not together*— a tasty weakness!

Anna relocated from New York to the Carolinas as a child. Her mother, a retired English and History teacher, always encouraged Anna's interest in writing, after discovering short stories she would write in her spare time.

As a child, she loved mysteries and checked out every *Encyclopedia Brown* story that came into the school library. Before too long, her fascination with history and reading led her to her first historical romance—Margaret Mitchell's *Gone With The Wind*, now a treasured, but weathered book from being read multiple times. The day she discovered Kathleen Woodiwiss,' books, *Shanna* and *Ashes In The Wind*, Anna became hooked. She read every historical romance that came her way and dreams of writing her own historical romances took seed.

Today, her focus is primarily the Regency and Civil War eras, although Anna enjoys almost any period in American and British history. She would love to connect with any of her readers on her website – www.annastclaire.com, through email – annastclaireauthor@gmail.com, Instagram – annastclaire_author, BookBub – www.bookbub.com/profile/anna-st-claire, Twitter – @1AnnaStClaire, Facebook – facebook.com/authorannastclaire or on Amazon – amazon.com/Anna-St-Claire/e/B078WMRHHF.

Made in United States
Troutdale, OR
06/26/2024